Jokes for the Gunmen

Jokes for the

Jokes for the Gunmen

Mazen Maarouf

Translated from the Arabic
by Jonathan Wright

GRANTA

Published by Granta Books in 2019

Granta Publications
12 Addison Avenue
London
W11 4QR

A CIP catalogue record for this book is available
from the British Library

9 8 7 6 5 4 3 2 1

ISBN 978 1 84627 667 5
eISBN 978 1 84627 669 9

www.granta.com

Contents

Jokes for the Gunmen

I *The Pepper Plant*

I DREAMED THAT MY FATHER HAD A GLASS EYE. When I woke up my heart was pounding like the heart of a frightened cow, but I was smiling and happy. For a moment I thought my dream had finally come true and my father really did have a glass eye.

When I was young, my father gave me a pepper plant for my birthday. It was a strange present. I didn't understand what it meant at the time. We could hear gunfire from time to time, but we grew used to it, as one grows used to the honking of passing cars. Just as I didn't understand what was happening in the neighbourhood, I didn't understand why my father had chosen a pepper plant or why the plant stayed with us. But the plant had two tiny peppers just forming, and I felt intuitively that they represented me and my twin brother. The gunmen fought around our street for months, because of its location between the sea and the city centre. But my mother still sent us to school – me and my twin brother, who was deaf, and on the way he would get frightened and stick close to me for protection.

I didn't like my father's present at the time. I found it odd and ugly. I didn't tell any of the other children at school about it. But I looked after it, as my father had asked me to. My father owned a laundry that did ironing and dry cleaning, and he taught me to wipe the little budding peppers with a piece of cotton and to light a candle over them so they would get vitamins and grow. He would wipe them very gently. 'You have to take care of them so that they produce more buds,' he told me. 'This pepper plant must become your friend.' My father's behaviour led me to believe that in every tiny pepper there was a soul that I had to protect at any cost. That was my little mission in the war, and sometimes, when the fighting was intense and the gunmen were using heavy weapons such as mortars and RPGs, my terrified mother and brother would lie flat on the floor in the corridor, between the sitting room and the kitchen and the bathroom, while I stood near the television, the part of the house most exposed to snipers, holding a candle to cast light over the pepper plant, in the belief that our souls – my soul, my brother's, my father's and my mother's – were also inside the tiny peppers, and that if I did this none of us would be in danger of being killed, especially my father, who didn't come home until the evening. That's how the close association between me and the pepper plant began, and I became more affectionate towards it, although at one stage I did stop giving it water, but spat on it instead. I would drink the water instead of giving it to the plant, because my mother said there was a water shortage and people were dying of thirst. I was frightened and started drinking that water, imagining that it would stop me getting thirsty in the future. I also felt that watering the pepper plant with my own saliva made me closer to it. But then my mother saw me doing it one day and told my father when he came home from work.

That was the first time my father whipped me with his belt. He was so angry I couldn't believe it. Did spitting on the pepper plant really call for all this anger, I wondered. I saw my deaf brother screwing up his eyes and trembling each time the belt landed on me. When my father went away, I went up to the pepper plant, sobbing, my eyes drowned in tears, and tried to work out which of the peppers held my father's soul. It was easy. I chose the biggest pepper, broke it off spitefully and crushed it under my foot.

2 *A Grasshopper*

AT SCHOOL THE KIDS COMPETED WITH EACH
other by telling stories about how their fathers beat
them. These stories illustrated the power each father had
in his household. Power was the most important subject,
as far as we were concerned, during the war. My father
wasn't at the top of the hierarchy of fathers, of course,
because he hadn't invented the cruellest punishment.
But I told the other kids boastfully that he had whipped
me with a leather belt. When I was asked why, I lied. I
didn't say it was because I had spat on the pepper plant.
Instead I made up a story that showed me doing something really daring, that showed I was made of heroic
stuff. 'I swallowed my mother's bottle of Valium pills,' I
said. 'And my father whipped me till I threw up the pills
all in one go.'

Some days after I told my heroic story, a friend of
mine came up to me and told me he'd seen my father

being beaten up in the street. 'He was wearing a brown belt,' he said, 'but he didn't use it. Isn't that the belt he whipped you with?' 'Yes,' I replied with a nod. Because my father only had one brown belt. My friend, who saw the whole scene, described it to me as if it were happening in a peep show he was watching. When my father came home, I noticed that the marks on his face were not scalds from the steam in the laundry; in order to find out how painful they were, I prodded the largest mark on his face with my finger. He was asleep, but he started from the pain and turned his face away without opening his eyes, pretending he was still asleep.

It was then that I realized that my father's soul had left the pepper plant for ever. I blamed myself, because if I hadn't broken off the largest pepper and trodden it underfoot, my father wouldn't have become so weak, or so cowardly either. That's what hurt me most.

My father didn't beat me after that, despite my repeated attempts to provoke him. I spat on the pepper plant several times in front of him, but he didn't react at all, no matter how big the glob of spit was or how noisily I did it.

My father stopped speaking to me so often. He started spending most of his time in the bathroom, sitting on the edge of the bathtub. I would snoop on him through the keyhole and he looked absent-minded.

He even started drooling at the mouth without realizing it. From behind the door – like a friend offering him advice as they fished, sitting side by side by the sea – I whispered through gritted teeth, 'Don't cry, don't cry.' And my father never did cry, which convinced me that he hadn't completely lost his grip.

A short while later, after he got back from work with footprints on his clothes, he picked up the television and put it under the tree in front of our building. There was nothing wrong with the television; my father just wanted everyone to see that that he wasn't watching anything political. My father never stopped going to work, because his laundry was responsible for washing and ironing clothes for the guests at a large hotel, most of them foreign journalists who had come from far away to write about the war that was going on in our street and in other nearby streets.

The story of my father being beaten up spread among the kids at school and, because of it, I was known as 'the grasshopper', on the grounds that my father was also a grasshopper, since grasshoppers always jump and never attack. I tried to defend myself against this slur by inventing stories about how my father beat me violently. On my way to school early in the morning, for example, I took to burning my arm or my stomach with cigarettes, or ripping my school uniform or scratching my own throat or eyes. I would go down some deserted alley and give myself a dose of self-inflicted morning torture. The pain was sometimes severe. And when I went into school like this, the kids would gather round me. Leaning on the gate and pretending to be a wreck, I would volunteer, 'It's my father. He beat me this morning. He's no grasshopper, like you think he is.' But the headmistress soon called me in. After examining me, she said, 'I have a feeling that you've done this to yourself,' on the grounds that no father would scratch his young son's neck while beating him or burn him with cigarettes and then send him to school. She summoned my mother, who came at once and laid into me with her fists as we were leaving school, within sight of the other kids, who were still in class; they crowded around the windows to watch and snicker like rats.

That was the first time I experienced failure. It made me willing to give up anything, even my little treasure trove of Matchbox cars, so that my father would become someone frightening. I was even willing to break open my money box, into which I had long whispered my dreams. I thought that whispering into the slot for the coins would make the money box fulfil all my wishes, because when you tell it your secret desires, it adjusts the amount of money inside – upwards, of course – so that it matches the cost of those dreams. My dream had been to buy one of those silver 6-mm pistols that at least three of the boys in the building possessed.

But now my dream was to get hold of a glass eye for my father.

3   *The* Sahlab *Seller*

THE IDEA OF THE GLASS EYE CAME FROM THE MAN who sold hot *sahlab* drinks at our school. I'd known from the start that I had to make a change to my father's face – sacrificing a part of his head to save the whole. But I didn't know how, or which part I should sacrifice. I would watch him at night when he was sleeping, examining his features and trying to work out what I could remove, or at least disfigure, to make him look frightening. But I didn't come to any conclusion. For a start, my father had a small face, and then it didn't help that he was such a light sleeper. My father was the kind of person who suddenly opens his eyes, looks at you in alarm, and then asks, 'Why haven't you gone to bed yet? Are you frightened?' So what could I possibly do? Whenever I saw him suddenly open his eyes, this was exactly the question that came into my head: 'Dad, are you frightened?' But, to smooth things over between us, I would say, 'No, Dad, we're not frightened, are we?'

'Of course not,' he would say in a low, hesitant voice. Then he'd walk me to my room so I could go back to sleep. He'd sit on the edge of the bed that my brother and I shared. He'd sit there, completely absent-minded, just as he sat on the edge of the bathtub. As soon as drool started dribbling from his mouth, I would shut my eyes, keeping the lids tightly closed and pretending I had nodded off. He would get up, go into the kitchen, drink some water and then get back into bed next to my mother, who always slept like a log.

The *sahlab* seller was a spy. He came to school twice a day. Completely bald, short and chinless, with just a thin moustache, he wore rubbish shoes, which made many of the children avoid buying *sahlab* from him. But apparently he didn't care. He kept coming to school, never saying anything. We never saw him speak. We also never saw him worked up. He would listen to your order, take the money from you and then give you your change if necessary. His right eye was missing, but that didn't put the children off. The rubbish shoes he wore made more of an impression – more than his eye. Disfigured bodies were a common sight in the war – as were adverts for imported cheese, which made you feel familiar with a cheese you would never taste – and it was also normal to see at least a dead body or two on television every day. Or one of the schoolkids would come and tell you in detail how one of his relatives had been killed by a shell. But to see a dead body wearing rubbish shoes? That was impossible. The *sahlab* seller was so shabby that he looked like a corpse, but none of the gunmen beat him up. Once, as I was buying a glass of *sahlab* from him outside the main school gate, I asked him, 'Have the gunmen ever beaten you up?' He didn't answer, so I raised my voice and said, 'Tell me, the gunmen – the gunmen who stand at the end of the street – have they ever beaten you up?' He shook his head without looking at me. When I saw his response, I felt a great happiness. 'Thank you,' I told him, assuming that this was definitely something to do with his missing eye.

4 *A Cardboard Box*

AFTER A WHILE I STOPPED GOING TO SCHOOL. IT was as if I had become a public toilet, where everyone deposited their shitty jokes. Especially after my mother slapped me in front of the other kids. I didn't feel guilty, and I didn't think about the consequences of staying away from school. In fact, I justified it to myself by saying I needed to have a rest and think about what could be done to help my father. I had to build up my relationship with the gunmen by any means possible – to become one of their associates. And in order to do that, I had to win their attention. Strike a blow. Boooom. Something to make them interrogate me. The very next day, I took my chance. I stole a cardboard box one of them had left on a ledge outside the building they had taken over. Inside the cardboard box there was a bag of lentils, some packets of pills and some doctor's prescriptions, a Peugeot car mirror and a piece of plastic whose function

I couldn't work out. The pills belonged to the mother of a low-level gunman. I picked up the cardboard box and ran off with it. The gunmen caught up with me. They didn't shoot at me because they managed to surround me near a parked car before they even had time to think about opening fire. I soon found myself in a room on the second floor of the gunmen's building. When the 'inter-rogation' (that's what I like to call it) began, I asked for a chair to sit on. A hand as heavy as a pigeon, or one and a half pigeons, came down on my neck. I coughed, as if to clear my throat, so that I wouldn't shed any tears. I hadn't brought myself to this place to be beaten up. Besides, slapping someone on the back of the neck, at least at school, meant the person was of no importance. If he was important, you would slap his face or punch him on the jaw or in the stomach. It was humiliating, but I stood up as straight as a glass, in an attempt to show my powers of endurance in the face of adversity. I wanted to win their admiration, but the only thing the gunmen's leader asked me, as he examined my school uniform and my satchel, was 'Are the schools closed today?' Before I could answer, the gunmen started asking each other the same question. Because if the schools were suddenly closed, it meant there had been some security develop-ment and they had to be on the alert. They hadn't heard this on the radio. Besides, the owner of the cardboard box I had stolen was just a wretched gunman whose job was to bring them coffee, tea and sandwiches. His mother was very ill and he had to go home to make her some lentil soup and give her her medicine, but my interrogation forced him to stay, and that's what upset him. He was the one who'd slapped me on the back of the neck.

I was thrown out of the building. My plan had been thwarted. I hadn't even been asked why I'd stolen the cardboard box. But I didn't go away. I didn't go home or go back to school. No, I stayed. I was there to make a deal with them. I was going to sell them my twin brother. At school I'd heard the bus driver talking to the woman who teaches science about these gunmen trafficking in human organs. Children's organs, to be precise. The problem for me was how to tell the gunmen who traffic in organs from those who don't. The bus driver didn't say anything about that to the teacher. When I went up to him and asked him, he said sarcastically, 'You can tell by asking them if they're organ fans.' But maybe he just wanted to impress the pretty teacher, so I had to ask the gunmen about it.

5   *The Deal*

I WAS HOLDING OUT HOPE THAT THE GUNMEN would be organ fans, because my deaf brother struck me as a hot commodity. Well, not one that was top-notch, I admit. The fact that his ears didn't work meant that part of him was missing. And that's because, apparently, my brother had used his ears so much when he had a fever that he no longer had any hearing. Besides, there were two of him – him and me. That would definitely bring the price down. But the price he would fetch, plus what was in the money box, would mean I could buy a glass eye for my father. And there was another reason that would definitely persuade the gunmen to buy him – my brother had two hearts.

Yes, that's what my mother said. She repeatedly said that children who have a disability, such as deafness, blindness, inability to speak or whatever, have a second heart. God takes one sense from them, but in its place

He gives them another heart on the right side of their chests, because there isn't enough room on the left-hand side. When we were little boys, we both had a fever, like any twins. When we got over it, I discovered that the fever had taken his hearing from my brother and given it to me. But I didn't tell him this. My ability to hear really did double, whereas he could no longer hear at all, and he no longer spoke to me much. He just smiled. That was because he had two hearts, and that's what I was betting on when I spoke to the gunmen. But I left the matter of the two hearts till the end. For the shock value. Like a shell that hits a bus full of disabled children. I said everything all in a rush.

I went up to the gunman and asked him, 'Are you organ fans?' In case he didn't say, 'Yes,' or in case he threw me out, I quickly added, 'I have a brother, and he wants to sell himself. My brother and I are one. He's the one who'll sell himself to you, but I'm the one who'll get the money. I don't want to cheat you. He can't hear and there are two of him – me and him – but my brother does have two hearts.'

The gunman looked at me and said, 'Two hearts? And you want us to traffic in organs? What do you know about human organs, you piece of shit?'

'Everything,' I lied.

'Everything? Then show me where your phallus is.'

'It's inside my body here,' I said, putting my hand on my hip, to the left of my belly button.

The gunman burst out laughing. In fact, I had long had a feeling that a person's phallus had something to do with their kidney, but I didn't know where exactly it would be. No one had told me that a phallus was the willy, as my father called it, that I piss through.

When he stopped laughing and could see how embarrassed I was – my face was as red as a beetroot – he said, 'Of course. Go and fetch your brother.'

I couldn't believe what I'd heard, and it didn't occur to me that the gunman was making fun of me. I walked off, thinking that if the deal went through, I would also get revenge for my father on the gunmen who had beaten him up. With the money I got from them, I would have him fitted with a glass eye that would give them the fright of their lives. Instead of going back home, I waited till it was time for the kids to come out of school. I was very happy and when I went in I found my brother and my mother as usual. He smiled at me. I took him to the bathroom, washed his face and asked him to open his mouth so that I could check his teeth. I also checked his ears and made sure they were clean. I heard my mother praying to God to preserve me. My brother didn't understand anything. I signed to him to say, 'We're off,' and then, 'Don't tell Mother.' He smiled, in that way that would make you think that he really did have two hearts.

I took my deaf twin brother along to the gunmen. Because he was deaf, my mother wouldn't let him out of the house, not even to let him play in front of the building. If clashes suddenly broke out, he wouldn't hear the noise and he would be an easy target for a sniper. 'I'm going to buy him something from the shop,' I said to my mother. She was happy, because I hadn't bought my brother a treat before. When we reached the gunmen's checkpoint, I said, 'Here he is!' and I pushed him forward a little. 'He looks just like me but he can't hear and he has two hearts, as I told you,' I said. But my brother had a feeling that something was up. He turned round and grabbed my shirt pleadingly. I could feel his grip, his fingers clamped tight. I realized he was frightened. He dug his heels into the ground like a little goat and looked at me. 'This is for Dad's sake,' I told him with signs.

'So you're here to sell your brother,' said the gunman.

'Yes, I'll sell him to someone else if we can't agree the terms,' I answered confidently.

'Since you're so serious, come and let's make a deal upstairs,' he said, gesturing to my brother to wait. When my brother saw me go into the building with the gunman, he burst into tears, but I waved to reassure him.

6 *My Deaf Brother*

THIS WAS THE ONLY TIME I WAS BEATEN UP BY THE gunmen. They weren't the same gunmen who left their footprints on my father's shirt, but I found out what it feels like to be trodden underfoot. On the way home, my brother felt sad for my sake. Halfway home he stopped me to touch my cheeks, as I had done with my father – my neck and cheeks had livid bruises. When he touched me, I dropped to the ground and turned my face away, pretending to be asleep. Then I let him help me stand up. When I got home, my mother freaked out as soon as she saw me. She started screaming and asked me what had happened. But I wasn't paying attention and, instead of going into the bathroom, sitting on the edge of the bathtub and drooling, I stood in front of the pepper plant and started to examine it. One of the little peppers had withered and shrivelled up. The sight greatly disheartened me. I told myself that the little pepper must be my little soul, which had been humiliated. The next day I didn't leave the house. I didn't pretend to go to school. I spent the day spraying water on the shrivelled pepper and blowing on it to revive it. But my attempts were in vain. In the middle of the day the little pepper dropped off and landed on the soil. My heart began to beat violently, like trampling feet. I didn't realize that the withered pepper didn't represent my soul but rather my brother's. That afternoon my brother's bus didn't come back from school. We found out later that a shell had hit it. My brother and all the other children in the bus were incinerated and their bodies fused with each other. They were buried together in a small, remote terraced field near the school.

My brother had been going to a special school for the deaf and dumb and the blind. His bus was something all the kids in the street liked to stare at, because, as far as they were concerned, the passengers were weird. The bus smelt of dough, bananas and milk, and it was my job to wait for it with my brother every morning. I hated that. As soon as my brother got on the bus, some of the kids would start pointing at me in amazement and laughing at the fact that I was an exact copy of him. My brother liked that. He was proud of the close resemblance between us. But I looked away, so that I wouldn't meet his eyes after he had boarded the bus. Then he would press his face against the windowpane and wave to me with a broad, stupid smile that I felt might become detached from his face and turn into a slimy toad that would jump on my nose.

7 Jokes for the Gunmen

AFTER MY BROTHER DIED, MY MOTHER STOPPED eating. She started smoking heavily and arguing noisily with my father, who continued to go to work in the laundry and kept getting beaten up by the gunmen. When he came back from work, he went into the bathroom, sat on the rim of the bathtub and drooled, even more than previously, but he never cried. In the meantime I looked at him and gritted my teeth. The reality is that I wasn't much affected by the loss of my brother, because the idea that there were two of him – him and me – and that only one of them was gone prevented me from feeling the shock. For me it was a half loss, or even a quarter loss, if we take into account the fact that I still had my brother's sense of hearing. I was still determined to press on with my project – buying a glass eye for my father. But I did resume going to school. My brother's death had restored my standing among the schoolkids. They stopped making fun of me, because it would have been improper to laugh at a classmate whose deaf brother had been blown up by a shell.

But things didn't improve for my father in the same way. The fact that he had lost his child made the gunmen realize that he was not only weak but also sad. Now, after giving him a thorough thrashing, instead of saying as usual, 'We're here to protect you,' they started asking him to tell them jokes. 'Come on, tell us a joke before you go. Take your time,' they would say. So my father would have to think of a joke. Of course, in front of a bunch of gunmen you have to be a good storyteller to win your freedom. Your story has to be convincing, enjoyable and very short, and it has to make people laugh. Not like this story, for example.

We started spending more time together, me and my father. Although it was still the period of mourning for my deaf brother, my father and I had to make up jokes together. Jokes for the week. A joke a day. Just for the gunmen. And every joke had to be sharp. And sometimes rude. My father said, 'Never mind. You can use rude words. What matters is the joke.' My mother couldn't take part in these evening sessions. Because she was the mother of the deceased boy, she was in the depths of despair, totally pale, silent and thin. My brother's death seemed to have hollowed her out.

I must admit that the jokes were not good. At least, they didn't make me laugh. Although I helped make them up, I didn't get most of them. My father, on the other hand, thought they fitted the bill. He would smile with relief whenever we finished making up a joke. It was as if the day was done and he could rip that page off the wall calendar. Sometimes we'd spend the whole night making up a funny story, and sometimes we'd have to wake up early, sit together at the kitchen table and confer in whispers as we tried to work out the punchline to a joke that needed one. Sometimes I'd turn to the older schoolkids for help. I'd ask them to tell me a joke that would make people laugh, make them laugh big-time, and they would come up with one, out of sympathy, believing that I urgently needed cheering up because I had lost my twin brother. They would tell me the latest jokes they had heard and I would pass them on to my father in the evening. Then we'd start adjusting them to make sure they were quite new and had never been heard before. But whenever we finished making up a joke, I noticed that my father looked older.

My father said that sometimes he had to tell the joke while the gunmen had the radio on, and when the news came on they would say, 'Shhh,' and my father would stop, wait till the end of the bulletin and then tell the joke again from the beginning. As soon as he got a detail of the joke wrong, he'd get a slap on his face and one of them would say, 'That's not exactly what you said the first time.' When the joke was over, they'd remind him that they were like brothers to him and if he needed anything he could come to see them, since they were there to protect us and help us. But I knew they were lying. If they really wanted to protect him, why hadn't they poked his eye out yet, I wondered. They must have realized that if my father had a glass eye fitted, he would frighten them.

8   *The Hippopotamuses*

I HAD TO ACT. MAKE A MOVE. IT WAS OBVIOUS MY
father would never get a glass eye if he went on like this.
I had to increase his chances by provoking the gunmen
to poke out one of his eyes, even if they came to regret
it later. Meanwhile my plan was to hire a bodyguard for
my father.

My brother and I used to save large banknotes in
our joint money box on a fifty-fifty basis. Sometimes I
would cheat, but not my brother. He didn't have any
opportunity, since I kept a close eye on him. Sometimes
I would search his trousers while he was asleep and, if I
came across a large banknote, I would keep it for myself.
My brother was sometimes given extra pocket money
because he was deaf, as if he could use the money to buy
a new sense of hearing. So as not to hurt my feelings,
he would hide it from me. But in the end I would find
it. When my brother couldn't find it, he didn't ask me

about it, and he didn't snitch on me to Mother or Father. He just smiled and pointed at me as if to say, 'I know.' I had forgotten about the money box since his death, but now I decided to use it. For the benefit of the family, of course. I was now going to school regularly. To study and to bring jokes for my father. I thought I could put off the matter of the glass eye for a short while.

There was always a group of young men standing near the school. Five or six of them. We used to call them the 'hippopotamuses'. They were brothers. All of them were tall, about the same height, and they were all equally massive. They were always well turned-out and walked in single file. They showered regularly, their hair was trimmed, their clothes were clean and they had gold chains around their necks. They were known to be quiet but also vicious, and they worked by the hour. I heard from the kids at school that they carried out difficult assignments, such as saving gunmen from certain tricky situations. Once they saved a sniper after the building where he was stationed on the roof was surrounded by hostile gunmen. So I wanted to make an agreement with the hippopotamuses. Not all of them, since one hippopotamus would be more than enough to protect my father.

I took the money box to school. After lessons were over and everyone had left, I walked towards the hippopotamuses, taking the green plastic money box out of my satchel. I didn't look at any of them – I just kept walking until I ended up standing in front of them. Or rather, in front of one of them. I had to speak rapidly and say everything without stopping. Without looking up at the face of the person I was speaking to, I said, 'Do you want a job I need a bodyguard for just one hour a day half an hour in the morning and half an hour in the evening and the money's in the box what do you say?' As I spoke I pushed my money box towards his stomach.

'Bodyguard? Who for? For you?'

'No, for my father.'

'And what does your father do?'

'He has a laundry.'

'And how much is there in the money box?'

'I don't know. Open it up at your place and tell me tomorrow how many hours you can work for the money inside it,' I said. My heart was pounding, because everything seemed to be going so well.

The next day the hippopotamuses came into school. That was during Maths. They knocked on the door, came in and asked me to come out to talk to them. Of course the teacher couldn't do anything, nor could the headmistress. In fact, because the hippopotamuses asked to speak to me personally, that earned me double respect among both the kids and the staff. Outside the classroom one of the hippopotamuses said to me, 'For the money in the money box, I can work seven hours. That means a week.'

'Seven hours? That's all?' I said confidently.

'Yes, and whether you agree or refuse now won't make any difference, because we take our fees in advance, whether I complete the job or not.'

'A week's fine, just fine. You'll escort my father for half an hour in the morning on his way to work and half an hour in the evening when he goes back home. You don't have to escort him literally. Just walk behind him. Keep a short distance between the two of you, and let other people know that you're his bodyguard, but don't speak to him.' Now I was talking like a gangster.

The man answered sharply, as if he'd been insulted, 'You do realize you're dealing with a professional here?'

It was Wednesday and we agreed that the man would start work the coming Monday, in five days' time, that is, because he was tied up with certain other operations.

9   *Father Abducted*

THE HIPPOPOTAMUS WAS A TRUE PROFESSIONAL
and a man of his word, like any ambitious gangster. On
the agreed Monday morning, my father found a man
waiting for him at the entrance to the building. The man
walked behind my father without uttering a word. Just as
a bodyguard does. The hippopotamus had several pistols
and several bullet belts draped over his shoulders. Despite
my young age, he carried out the mission I had assigned
him to the letter. I could see that for myself. I was
peeking from behind the curtain. The distance between
him and my father was very small. My father was terrified
and didn't dare speak to this enormous stranger. In fact,
he was so frightened that he stopped halfway and threw
up his breakfast on the pavement. As a professional, the
hippopotamus stopped too and, while waiting for my
father to finish vomiting, looked around in all directions,
checking the pavements, the buildings and the roadway.

When my father reached the laundry, the body-guard disappeared from sight. But my father remained apprehensive and tense all day long and had pains in his stomach. When he set about closing up the laundry at a quarter to nine in the evening, when the television news ended, the nightmare began again and the man walked behind my father to the entrance of our building. The gunmen didn't accost my father that day, maybe because they didn't want any trouble with the hippopotamuses. The next day my father didn't leave the house. He didn't even leave his room. He didn't look out of the window till noon, and the hippopotamus wasn't there then, which reassured him.

But the process was repeated on the third day and, halfway to the laundry, my father could no longer keep walking. He stopped and hailed a taxi. But then he found the hippopotamus sitting beside him in the back seat. 'Have I done anything bad?' my father asked him in a trembling voice.

'I don't know. I've been hired to escort you,' answered the bodyguard.

'Hired? Who hired you?'

'Do you have a son in the first grade of middle school?'

'Yes.'

'He was the one who hired me.'

My father didn't come home that day. When the hippopotamus bodyguard got to the laundry a little before 8.45 p.m., he found it shut. My mother stayed up all night waiting for my father, but there was no trace of him. I had to stay awake next to my poor mother. My eye was hurting badly and I took a tablet. But there was one idea jumping around in my head like a squirrel: was it possible my father had been kidnapped? Early in the morning, we heard knocking on the door. We thought it was Father, but when my mother opened the door she found the hippopotamus standing in front of her. He was upset that an ordinary man had managed to elude him. He asked to speak to me. 'Listen, kid,' he said. 'I consider this to be breach of contract. Tell that to your father.' Then he left.

I knew the hippopotamuses could find my father if I asked them to. It would cost a lot of money, of course. But my mother was willing to pay as much as the laundry was worth in order to get him back. I preferred to have my father out of the way for a while, because I had always wanted him to be famous for his role in the war – and this was his chance. Given that my father was out of sight, he must have been kidnapped. That was the story I would put about. That would give the impression that his kidnappers saw my father as a man of consequence, the opposite of what my mother kept saying for the neighbours to hear – that Father was innocent, that he had never even bought a newspaper, and that he had no opinion on what was happening in the country. In fact, she swore repeatedly that the gunmen were constantly beating him up and that he was a completely willing victim.

My mother wanted my father back whatever it might cost, but I never made it clear to her that we could get him back whenever we wanted by employing the hippopotamuses. At school I noticed that the kids had become more sympathetic towards me. I was now the kid who had lost his deaf brother and whose father had been kidnapped. Maybe there was another reason for their sympathy too, but I did feel relieved. I smiled all the time and was boastful, because at last my father had won recognition in the annals of the war as someone who'd been kidnapped. His picture had even been published in the newspaper, which annoyed the gunmen, who were jealous because their pictures had never appeared in any newspaper. Then his name was mentioned on television, among the names of people who had gone missing that month. Meanwhile at school, I wrote in my essays about the military plans he drew up at home, his orders to gunmen who came around to our house, and his deep and secret friendship with the hippopotamuses.

But two months after he disappeared we received a

legal notification from a lawyer, informing us that my father had bequeathed me the laundry and all its equipment and coat hangers. Obviously it would have been impossible for someone who'd been kidnapped to hire a lawyer from his place of captivity, so my mother and I realized that Father was alive and well, that he hadn't been kidnapped and hadn't come to any harm. He had just left home of his own free will. The news hit me like a thunderbolt, but my mother's mood took a turn for the better. The next day I didn't go to school. I was too embarrassed. I never went back. A short while later I decided to devote my time to washing and ironing people's clothes in the little laundry.

10 *A Phone Call*

I NEVER SAW MY FATHER AGAIN. HE DOES CALL ME
sometimes – he rings me on the laundry phone twice a
week, to check up on me and my mother and to ask how
business is. I answer him in a roundabout way: 'Business
is fine, Dad. I'm thinking of opening another branch.
We miss you, Dad. Won't you come and visit us?' I beg
him to tell me where he's living. But he refuses, every
time. Now he's remarried and he has twin boys. He tells
me about them and how they look like we looked, my
brother and I, when we were their age. Although it's
fifteen years since he left, my father still feels ashamed.
He says he feels embarrassed. 'What a coward I was!' he
says. 'It's OK, Dad, in war not everyone can be brave,' I
reply. I look in the mirror while I'm speaking to him on
the phone. Always. I don't tell him that I always wanted
him to have a glass eye, because that would be painful
for both of us. Then he asks me the same old question,

the question he never forgets in any phone call: 'How's your eye, your glass eye?' 'It's fine, Dad,' I reply. 'It's completely adapted to my face. I can even blink normally. You should see it.' 'That's good to hear. It was a dire day, that Wednesday. Do you remember? You shouldn't have stayed at school after class.'

'Yes, Dad. I remember the day well. It really was an unlucky day. I even owe you an apology,' I say.

'An apology? Don't be silly. I should be apologizing to you and your mother.'

I had stayed behind at school, determined to make an agreement with the hippopotamus about a new idea that would only take a few minutes to put into effect. After the hippopotamuses visited our class, it had occurred to me that, instead of hiring one of them as a bodyguard, I should ask them to poke out my father's eye. When the school bell rang for the end of lessons, I couldn't find the hippopotamuses anywhere, so I stayed behind to wait for them. Some of the kids were still in the playground. They were playing dodgeball with a tennis ball. In dodgeball two boys throw a ball back and forth and try to hit a group of boys standing half way between them. I joined them, but I wasn't concentrating fully. As I played I was thinking about the hippopotamuses and the new plan. Suddenly the ball hit me in the eye. I lost consciousness immediately and when I came round I was in hospital.

I opened my right eye and my mother and father were standing near the bed. My left eye was bandaged up, my head was hurting badly and I felt slightly dizzy. My father smiled and stroked my hair, then told me what was going to happen in a while in the operating theatre. 'You're a big boy and from now on you won't be just a boy. You'll be a man.' Then he took something wrapped in a surgical dressing out of his pocket and unwrapped it to show a small ball. It was a plastic version of the glass eye that was going to fill the hole in my face. The iris was the same colour as my own. The whiteness was also an approximate match.

Whenever he calls me, we go over the incident together. We also remember the pepper plant. I tell him it's grown. It only grows peppers in two places – two peppers every year. The first one always appears where it's meant to be, representing my mother's soul. The second one grows where the one representing my father's soul used to be, but whenever I look at it closely I have a feeling that it carries my soul. My father tells me that he's been dreaming about me. It's the same dream every time, in which the doctors replace my glass eye with a natural one. They restore my real eye. Then we laugh. 'Don't tell me it's the same dream again,' I say, and he swears by his twin sons that it was the identical dream. We laugh and I wipe a tear from my good eye.

I wear glasses now and they make my glass eye look bigger. It looks really frightening. Then I add in jest, 'If war breaks out again, I'll have a face that frightens people.'

'Maybe that's for the best. Best for both of you.'

Matador

MY UNCLE DIED THREE TIMES IN THE SPACE OF one week. He began his death marathon on the Tuesday, right after he came back from the slaughterhouse. 'I've been cheated,' he said, and lay down on the sofa and died. I wasn't there when this happened, but Mother told me about it later. My uncle had been wearing his Spanish matador suit and it was spattered with white cow saliva. Apparently they had laughed at him at the slaughterhouse, so he'd taken off the suit and hung it in the wardrobe before lying down on the sofa and dying.

That was the first time my uncle died, and of course we treated him as a corpse. We kept him in the sitting room until it was his turn to be buried. They told us that luckily we would only have to wait two days. The sitting room is the only room in the house with air conditioning. It's also the smallest room. When you put the air conditioning on full you feel like an ant that's swallowed a pin and can no longer move.

Personally I like it when we put the air conditioning on, because we only do it on special occasions. Then you'll see me in my cotton pyjamas with a hood, punching the air as if I'm boxing a giant crane. I got that idea from Rocky in the film. That's also what I did with my uncle's body. I started punching it. Just on the soles of his feet, mind you. But apparently the punches pumped the blood from his feet to his heart and he came round. That's the deepest analysis I've managed to make but I haven't let on to anyone. Would you expect me to tell Mother that I punched my dead uncle's feet? Even my uncle didn't know I'd punched him. As soon as he came round, which was on the Thursday morning, he rubbed his foot and removed a thorn. He said the thorn kept hurting his soul and that meant he couldn't die peacefully. His body hadn't been washed yet and he hadn't had his fingernails trimmed. He took a shower and cut his nails.

My uncle had long wanted to be a bullfighter, but he could never afford the airfare to Mexico or Spain. And besides, he had to get a visa. He had tried at both embassies and each time he wrote that his aim was not to immigrate but just to be a matador. But his applications were rejected three times and he was told he no longer had the right to submit visa applications. Someone suggested he buy a bullfighter's suit. It took him four years to pay off the instalments. The suit had belonged to Luis Miguel Dominguín, the famous Spanish bull-fighter. At least, that's what he was told, but no one other than my uncle believed the story. He would sniff the suit and say, 'This is definitely Dominguín's suit. In it I can smell the souls of all the bulls he slew.' Anyway, my uncle would put on the outfit and practise in the slaughter-house, picking cows that were on their way to slaughter. He'd leave home at two o'clock in the morning and come back at dawn. The slaughterhouse would be full of traders, butchers and tough guys skilled with knives and cleavers. When their turn to be slaughtered came, the cows would wait in a small courtyard, while the men prepared to tie them in chains and hoist them up. Then my uncle would move in, smartly dressed in his golden suit, his hair, covered in gel, as shiny as his shoes. Then the betting would open.

My uncle would choose the largest cow, pounce on it and strangle it with his bare hands – my uncle had hands as big as those old telephone receivers people used to have at home. As soon as the cow was about to breathe its last, one of the slaughtermen would come forward and finish the job by making a slit in the cow's throat.

It was no secret that sometimes my uncle got carried

away by his own strength and strangled the cow to death. Then the cow would be no good for halal meat and he would have to pay for it. But what people didn't know was that my uncle arranged in advance with one of the apprentices that the night before the cow was slaughtered the boy would beat its legs with a stick until the legs swelled up. That way it was easy for my uncle to knock the cow to the ground.

My uncle was a cheat. When he was cheated in turn and a cow defeated him, he felt humiliated and died. Of course any matador who's defeated by a cow is bound to feel very humiliated. But my uncle recovered his self-confidence and his fearlessness after he came back to life. The little thorn that had been stuck in the bottom of his foot was the reason for that. He explained to us that when he was dead he had seen himself on a matadors' ranch in heaven. He was surrounded by all the champion bullfighters. He had even seen a bullring, he said. But he didn't understand anything because they were speaking Spanish. But God brought him back to life so that he could remove the thorn from his foot. 'A matador can't fight a bull if he has a thorn stuck in his foot,' God told him. When he pulled it out he was overcome with joy. It was enough that God had accepted him as a matador. My uncle saw it as testimony to his talent for bullfighting, even though he had never fought a bull in his life. As a result my uncle confidently took the matador suit out of the wardrobe to wear again. He said he would never take it off: he would go into the slaughterhouse wearing it and take on the biggest cow there, this time without any cheating. If God had endorsed his dreams, why should he care about the riff-raff at the slaughterhouse? But a surprise lay in wait for him. When my uncle tried on the matador suit again, he found it was too big for him. No one could explain why that should be. It caused consternation at home, by raising the possibility that my uncle was in fact still dead. The suit was baggy, and that was very strange. Dead bodies are meant to inflate, so their clothes should be tighter, not looser. But in my uncle's case it was the other way round.

My uncle died on the Tuesday and came back to life on the Thursday, only to find that his suit was too baggy, although he hadn't lost an ounce of weight. He couldn't wear the suit or go back to the slaughterhouse to tell the 'rabble', as he called them, what had happened to him in the matadors' ranch in heaven. Now he had to eat to put on weight. But our house was poor. He had an argument with Mother. He disconnected the air-conditioning unit and forced her to sell it and spend the money on food. Mother loves my uncle – he's her brother, one year younger than her, and he's been the man of the house since Dad died. She never denies him anything. It was then that I found out that I could no longer wear my cotton pyjamas or box with anyone. I ended up objecting to Mother, 'What if he goes and dies again?' My uncle was sitting opposite me. He flew into a rage and hit me about the face and neck. I didn't cry. I stood facing him, defiant as a young bull without horns. A calf. He was half-dead as far as I was concerned. I felt a perverse pleasure in my arms and legs because I had punched my uncle's feet when he was dead the first time.

Now I wanted to punch him all over. I wanted to hide in the belly of the next big cow he'd choose and as soon as he put his hands on its neck I'd burst out of its throat like a jack-in-the-box and punch him in the face so hard that his nose came off and fell on the floor. But none of that came about.

Mother sold the air-conditioning unit on the Friday and bought two fat chickens, nuts, eggs and various kinds of fruit, vegetables and grains, as well as a large bag of rice and some milk. She spent the whole day in the kitchen, and in the evening she laid out a big meal for my uncle, as if he wouldn't have any food in heaven.

Usually my uncle only ate a little, like any matador. But that evening he stuffed the food greedily into his mouth, like a bull tasting apples for the first time. The sight of him chewing and swallowing the food disgusted me, so I looked away. Mother kept telling him, 'Eat up, brother.' But suddenly my uncle choked on the food, stopped breathing and died. It's true that I was sitting at the same table but I didn't turn towards him. I just heard him choking and dying, with my mother saying, 'Breathe, brother,' and sobbing. My uncle had turned into a corpse a second time. This time we carried him to the hospital mortuary because there was no air conditioning in the sitting room. We managed to pay for one night in the mortuary with the money left over from selling the air-conditioning unit.

The next day, the Saturday, as part of the funeral procession from the mortuary to the cemetery, some of the slaughtermen wanted to take his body into the courtyard of the slaughterhouse, where he had performed his exploits and built his reputation. Mother agreed, on the condition that we call in at the house so that she could dress him up in the matador suit.

I thought this was silly, because the suit was too baggy for him and people would make fun of his appearance. I said this to Mother, but she whispered, 'I'll deal with that. Anyway, no one looks too closely at the size of the clothes dead people wear in their coffins.'

Mother asked me to help dress my uncle in the matador suit, to preserve his dignity. It was very hard to do, because his body was heavy and the sitting room was hot without the air conditioning. We put him in a sitting position, completely naked. I was about to lift his arm when he started to come round. 'What are you doing, you monkey?' he said. His repeated deaths had made him bad-tempered. Grouchy. When he realized that Mother was dressing him in the matador suit and planned to lower him into his grave, he was angry. He insulted her and pushed her away, and she fell over. I didn't like seeing my mother being mistreated, because she had good intentions. But I was worried he might lay into me, so I kept silent. 'Do you want the matador guys in heaven to make fun of me?' he said.

We told the people waiting outside that my uncle had come back to life, and they dispersed. Some of them were annoyed and asked us not to tell them next time my uncle died, because they thought they had done their duty by taking part in the funeral procession already.

My uncle stayed with us from the Friday to the Sunday and died in the slaughterhouse at dawn on the Monday morning. He had lost hope of gaining enough weight to fit in the suit. The story of the baggy suit had leaked out – I don't know how. Probably it was Mother. Mother always had good intentions. She had spoken to a seamstress, who was her friend, asking if there was any way the suit could be taken in. The seamstress said, 'No,' and let out the secret. The whole slaughterhouse found out. They made fun of my uncle. He went to the slaughterhouse wearing the baggy suit. He went into the courtyard and they let out the biggest cow. My uncle couldn't control it because he was tripping up on the suit, and the cow trampled him and he died. We buried him, crushed and bloodied, on Tuesday morning, a week after his first death. Only a few people attended the burial.

Mother washed the matador suit and asked me to dispose of it. We needed the money, so I sold it at the Sunday market for second-hand clothes. I laid out some plastic sheeting that Mother had lent me and arranged the suit on top in three pieces – the trousers, the shirt and the jacket. My uncle had never owned matador shoes or underwear. I had no other items for sale and I had to sell the suit at any price. But I was lucky, as people soon started gathering.

In the end a foreign man came up and started examining it. Then he asked me in broken Arabic, 'Where you get this suit?' I was worried. He added, 'This is Dominguín's suit, the famous matador's.' He gave me a large sum for it and with the money I was able to buy an air-conditioning unit and boxing gloves as well. I gave the rest of the money to Mother. My cotton pyjamas were waiting for me to wear them again, and I said to Mother, 'If I die, dress me in my pyjamas, and don't forget to put my boxing gloves on.'

Gramophone

ABU ELIA'S BAR WAS THE CHEAPEST IN BEIRUT during the siege. It was one level below ground. Long and narrow, it was shaped rather like a rectangular biscuit. But it was safe, or at least it was rumoured to be safe. Its walls were said to be made of reinforced concrete, not that anyone ever tried to check. Abu Elia had set up a stand with postcards in the bar and sometimes, during the evening or at the height of the shelling, some of his foreign customers would take a postcard and start writing on it blithely, as if they were at a picnic. Abu Elia would make sure it was sent to the post office the next day.

My father was the gramophone operator in the bar. That was his job. He spent hours and hours standing behind the bar, turning the handle of a Berliner gramophone from 1900 – there was no electricity and the bar was usually lit by candles. Sometimes he turned the handle slowly, because he was tired, and if a shell landed nearby, he might lose concentration and turn it faster, which would distort the music. But none of the customers paid any attention, because the sound from the gramophone was so faint it could hardly be heard anyway. What interested them was not so much the music it played but its age and the fact that it was manual. If you wanted to listen to a song you had to go up to the bar. The gramophone was my father's; he had inherited it from my grandfather, and had played it when he was young. He had been friends with Abu Elia since their school days and had suggested putting it in Abu Elia's bar. My father was like a DJ. He came home at dawn and, if I was awake, he would ask me to massage his arms. I liked that. He always fell fast asleep while I was massaging his strong arms.

Abu Elia's bar was only hit once, by a vacuum bomb that struck the whole building. The shell cut through three floors before exploding and crushing the building like an overripe pear. My father was one of the victims of course. Where he was, behind the gramophone player at the end of the bar, it would have been impossible to escape. The bomb sucked out all the air when it exploded but my father went on turning the handle of the gramophone for a moment, puzzled that the sound had completely disappeared. He was totally confused.

He wasn't even sure that his arm was really moving. For a moment he thought I hadn't massaged his arm properly at dawn the day before and he cursed me. Then he started to suffocate and the walls and ceiling folded in on top of him.

But my father didn't die. He came out of the bombing alive. No one had expected him or any of the people who lived in the building or who happened to be in the bar at the time to survive. He was the only one, saved by the gramophone, which was crushed of course. He told me later that just before the building collapsed some of the customers were gathered around him, examining the gramophone and listening to the faint sound it made. Before they met their doom, they were drinking beer and making jokes about my father and his gramophone.

The people in the bar died faster than they might have done, because there were no chairs in the place. Another unusual feature of Abu Elia's bar was that five of the eight brands of beer it served were sometimes of dubious authenticity. When I reached the building, I didn't know my father was still alive. There were four or five ambulance men there. They were volunteers. One of them asked me, 'Can you identify your father's body?' 'Definitely,' I replied, without thinking. 'Then make your way through the rubble and when you find it, point it out to me,' he said. I walked in. There was a smell of dead people mixed with beer, and the bodies were soaked. Even the rats hadn't survived. They had suffocated too and their eyes were bloodshot. The beer froth was still fresh and was seeping between the blocks of stone. These were not the best kind of dead people as far as those ambulance men were concerned. They were people who had died while drinking alcohol and it was not going to be fun digging them out.

I recognized my father's body from the arm I used to massage. The fingers were still clenched around the small handle of the gramophone. That made me smile. My father was as obstinate as a mule, although he was usually good-natured. I pointed out my father to the ambulance man and we pulled his body out together. It was easy to free it, despite the massive amount of rubble. The ambulance man, who was wearing a white mask, said, 'Boy, you're lucky. We won't be able to recover some of the bodies until the bulldozers arrive this evening.' I left my father's body in the ambulance. The ambulance man refused to let me take the gramophone handle. My father's arms were completely caked in blood and were like punctured tubes. I went to tell my mother. I was sixteen years old.

On the way home I swallowed my own vomit twice and when I arrived I had wrenching pains in my guts. I went into the bathroom and vomited. The vomit tasted very acidic and the acidity seemed to have damaged my throat or my oesophagus, because some blood came out too. That made me think of the pain my father must have felt when his arms lost all that blood I had seen.

In the hospital we were told that my father hadn't died, but he had lost both his arms. He was in bed, with those broad shoulders of his, rather like a robot super-hero whose arms had been cut off after a brutal battle with villains. But as soon as he came around from the anaesthetic he asked me in a frail voice, 'Where's the gramophone?'

'It got smashed, papa. There's nothing left of it,' I said.

He looked at his amputated arms, as if the loss of the gramophone had reminded him that disaster had also struck his own body. 'So I don't need my arms anyway,' he joked.

While my mother was wiping away her tears, I was summoned to the hospital reception desk, where I was given the gramophone handle and signed my name on a piece of paper. That was all that was left of the old machine. But my father changed shortly after he came back home. He had suffered some psychological damage. I hid the gramophone handle from him and didn't mention it to him. He just stared at my arms and my mother's arms, without looking at our eyes or faces. He spoke to us only through our arms. He focused his gaze on them so much that you felt that your hand was smeared with shit or that there was something wrong with it, and you had to put your hands in your pockets immediately, or hide your arms completely inside your sweater, leaving the sleeves hanging empty, like when we played at being beggars on the stairs as kids.

He would sometimes ask us questions such as: 'How do you feel when you look at me? Tell me honestly. How do you feel? Isn't it a privilege to have two arms? And your mother? She must feel the same way, mustn't she?' Sometimes he would ask me to move my arms in a particular way. 'Lift your arm up high, and then drop it down as if it's dead,' he would say. And I would reply, 'Stop that, Dad.' Or he would ask me to stand behind him and let my arms hang down so that my arms looked like they were his arms. Standing like this, we would move together to the mirror and he would take a long look at his own reflection, which now had my arms. 'Your arms fit my body perfectly, don't they? No wonder we're father and son,' he would say. This was painful to me. I had to obey him, as if I were still a child. My father started to become very irritable. As for my mother, she felt she was being punished, because my father had stopped sleeping with her but she couldn't abandon him.

'People would start talking, gossiping. They would see me as a bad woman,' she said.

My father also made a point of shitting and pissing in bed, so my mother started buying nappies for him and making him wear them. She washed his balls and ass, and shaved his beard with an electric razor because he didn't trust her with a razor blade in her hand. My attempts to convince him that he should trust her didn't succeed. 'Your mother used to have a lover when I worked in the bar,' he said. 'You don't know anything.'

In the end my father and I fell out, and since then we haven't exchanged a single word. My father had seen a medical programme on television about limb transplants, for arms and hands, for example. He called me into his room, which he never left. When I came in, he said meekly, 'I'm going to make a request that no father has ever asked of his son. If you agree, you'll gain everyone's respect – relatives, your friends and the neighbours. Everyone in the neighbourhood will respect you if you do this for me.'

'Of course, Dad,' I replied. 'You know I'd be willing to do anything.'

I had left school after my father had the accident and I'd worked as a carpenter's apprentice. Now I was a partner with two friends in a furniture factory, and I was ready to do everything in my power to fulfil my father's wishes.

'I want you to donate one of your arms to me,' he said. 'They said on television that it's medically possible.'

I couldn't believe that my father was asking me for an arm. I said nothing. I was thinking of that vacuum bomb and the gramophone. I wished I had lost my arms instead of him, and at that very moment, as if he could read my thoughts, my father said, 'If you had lost your arms, I would donate one of my arms to you without hesitation. What's an arm worth compared to me seeing you happy, or you seeing me happy?'

'I agree with you that this is a request no father has ever asked of his son,' I said. 'It's totally *original*,' I added, pronouncing the last word in the French style in a tone that was both sarcastic and sad. I tried to convince him that it was impossible: 'What if the operation was a failure? Then I would have lost my arm.'

He exploded with rage in my face. He said I was selfish and that even if the worst came to the worst, I would still have one arm. 'One arm is better than absolutely nothing,' he said.

I left the room and thought it over. I felt sad for my father. I didn't feel angry or disappointed. I was just sad and I told my mother. I was about to accept, because I no longer needed to use my arms in the furniture factory. I only supervised the designs and sometimes suggested some modifications. I could even employ an assistant.

My partners wouldn't object. But my mother implored me, 'Don't listen to him. Please don't listen to him. I'm willing to spend the rest of my life putting nappies on him, cleaning up his shit, shaving him and putting up with every indignity from him, but I will not see you losing one of your arms.'

After that my father refused to speak to me. He was resentful, but he continued to hope, very arrogantly, that one day I would change my mind, burst into his room and say, 'OK, Dad. I agree. Off we go to France together to have the operation.'

By now I was travelling to Paris often to visit my girl-friend. My visits were brief but relaxing, because I was far from home, where the atmosphere was poisoned by my father's deteriorating state of mind and the sadness of my mother, who was now prey to diabetes, high blood pressure and an irregular heartbeat.

Once my girlfriend gave me a music box with a little crank handle. When you turned it with two fingers it played '*Non, je ne regrette rien*' by Edith Piaf. I still had the gramophone handle in Beirut and when I came home from my trip, it occurred to me to connect the handle to the crank of the little music box. That's what I did. I thought of giving my father the music box with the handle of the gramophone player as a birthday present, in the hope that he might forgive me. But I changed my mind. It would probably irritate him. But my father found the music box and managed to take it into his room. Somehow he put it on the bedside table among the packets of pills that he took. He didn't say anything. He just put the music box with the gramophone handle on the bedside table. Of course he couldn't operate it and he didn't ask my mother to operate it for him. Maybe he was only interested in the handle, and maybe he kept the box and the handle together because he couldn't disconnect the handle from the box.

The whole thing was embarrassing. For the first time I felt guilty. Firstly, for keeping the handle for the twenty-three years since the accident without telling him, and then for deciding to connect the handle to the music box from France, the country where my father had long wanted to have one of my arms transplanted. I think it hurt him. My father didn't eat for days and fell into a decline. He was seventy-two years old by then. I went into his room. He had turned quite yellow. We called a doctor, who examined him quickly and told us his pulse was weak and he only had hours to live. He put him on a drip and said, 'It's for the best. Who knows what might happen?' Then he left.

There was nothing I could do. I sat next to him on the edge of the bed and picked up the music box with the gramophone handle, which was the last thing my father's hand had touched before his arm was cut off. I started to turn it. I wanted him to hear the music in the box before he passed away. I saw his lips move to make a feeble smile.

But he didn't revive. He just smiled. As he did so, I had the impression that his arms were growing slowly from their stumps, like mushrooms, their stalks pushing up from the ground after a heavy weight, such as a hat full of padlocks, has been removed. That encouraged me and I started turning the handle faster and faster. My heart was pounding. I wanted his arms to grow, to be fully grown, as if the vacuum bomb had never fallen and my mother had not spent her whole life putting nappies on him, and he was no longer lying beside this little music box, waiting for something to happen, something unique.

Cinema

IT ALL HAPPENED ON THE FIFTH DAY AFTER WE took shelter in the cinema. The food had almost run out and we were reduced to eating yellow triangles of processed cheese. At one o'clock in the afternoon Mother would take a wedge of cheese out of our teddy bear's tummy and divide it in half. I would eat one half and my sister would eat the other half, our heads hidden under the velvet cinema seats so that the other children, who were just as hungry as us, wouldn't see us. We didn't tell anyone there were seven wedges of cheese in the teddy bear's tummy.

At eight in the evening Mother would take another wedge of cheese out of the bear's tummy, and my sister and I would eat it in the same way and then go to sleep. Dozens of families had taken shelter in the cinema because it was three floors below ground level.

On the first day the families spread themselves out

over all the seats but the shelling grew more intense every day and every now and then people would move a little further down, away from the higher seats towards the lower ones. When one of the occupying army's tanks shelled the projection room at the top end of the auditorium, most of the families gathered on the stage and hid behind the curtain. The dividing line between us and the outside world was then the small wall that separated the projection room from the auditorium. The children could see daylight through the rectangular opening through which the film was usually projected.

Sometimes we would see Crazy Kimo go past outside. Kimo never took refuge anywhere throughout the war. He wasn't welcome in any of the shelters. It was said that he'd gone mad because he still had a piece of shrapnel in his body – no one knew exactly where. From the stage in the cinema you could see the empty street. If you stood at the edge of the curtain, a very small piece of the big wheel at the fairground was visible. The bottom corner of the curtain was the favourite place for children and they hung out there all day long.

On the fifth day a shell fell on the cinema, among the seats. I don't remember all the details. The blast threw me off the stage onto one of the seats in the auditorium. When I opened my eyes, I couldn't move and the seat was back to front, facing the road instead of the screen.

The other strange thing was that the wall between the projection room and the auditorium had not been knocked down. When I tried to see where the shell that landed in the cinema had come from, I couldn't work it out. There wasn't a hole anywhere. My sister's teddy bear was now in my arms, but my sister was nowhere to be seen. Nor was my mother, nor any of the other children or their families. The teddy bear was full of pieces of yellow cheese, but now there were also pieces of cheese of another brand that I had never seen before.

I called out for my sister: 'Sister, come on, let's share a wedge of cheese, or let's have two – a whole one for you and a whole one for me, because Mum's not here.' But she didn't appear. I didn't get up from the seat. I didn't have any reason to get up. The cinema seat was nice and warm. It smelt as if it was stuffed with millions of grains of soft sand, all connected to each other by threads. Very fine threads. I even thought about taking the seat with me to the grave and, instead of being buried lying down, being buried sitting in the cinema seat. I don't know why this idea occurred to me. I felt very much at ease. There was peace and quiet in the cinema.

On the morning of the next day I saw the cow. I was still sitting in the seat and the cow walked through the projection room. It stopped for a few moments. It lowered its head and looked at me through the rectangular hole and then continued on its way. The cow was big and beautiful. I looked around for my sister or one of the other children so that I could draw their attention to the cow, but the cinema was empty. I tried to get up from the seat but I couldn't. The teddy bear was weighing on my stomach and I couldn't budge it. It was heavy. I wondered whether that was because of the triangles of yellow cheese in its belly. I unzipped the teddy bear and took out a piece of cheese. I divided it in half. I ate one half in a single bite and held the other half in the air. I was hoping my sister would see it and would emerge from her hiding place and come over to me. She might be sitting in one of the seats behind me, and she might be hungry like me. My sister didn't appear, so I ate the other half of the piece of cheese. It didn't fill me up. I took another wedge out of the teddy bear's tummy and ate it, then a third and a fourth. I couldn't stop eating. I was hungry and the pieces of cheese were really delicious, even the kind I had never tasted before. I ate several triangles all in one go but I still wasn't full.

I tired of eating pieces of cheese and I dozed off, sitting in the cinema seat. The strange thing was that all the seats were still facing in the right direction except for the seat I was sitting on, which had its back to the screen and faced the projection room high up at the back.

The same thing happened again the next morning. The cow appeared and looked at me through the rectangular hole in the projection room, then it went on its way. I must admit that I was curious about the cow. What would a cow be doing in the projection room, I wondered. It occurred to me that the army had let it loose to spy on the people staying in the cinema. I didn't know anything about cow behaviour. But I found I wanted to follow it, because it was the first cow I had ever seen in real life.

The teddy bear was lighter now, because I had eaten several of the wedges of cheese in its tummy. I quickly unwrapped three more wedges and stuffed them into my mouth one after another. They tasted different now – less tasty than before. The cheese was sticky and upset my stomach. Now they tickled the roof of my mouth and I felt I was going to be sick, but I swallowed them like medicine. I tried to get up from the seat and only managed it with a great effort, in order to follow the cow. I left the auditorium and walked behind it. The cow wasn't in any great hurry; it was walking at a very leisurely pace, picking its way with difficulty because of the debris scattered everywhere. Despite that, it seemed completely at ease, as if it knew where it was going. I was struck by how clean it was, as if it were a house cat rather than a cow. But every now and then it would stop, bend its head and eat something that had just fallen from up above. I couldn't see what the cow was eating, but I could tell that it was hungry. The teddy was in my hands – I thought I had left it on the cinema seat – and once again it was full of wedges of cheese, as it had been ever since the cinema had been shelled. I took out a piece and threw it as hard as I could towards the hungry cow, in case it wanted to eat it. I hadn't unwrapped it and I wasn't sure that the cow would be able to unwrap it with its teeth, but I threw it anyway. Although the wedge of cheese was small, it didn't go very far. It landed one or two paces away from me. The cow paid it no attention at all. I took out another piece, unwrapped it this time, and threw it. It also landed only a metre or two away from me. It was as if I'd thrown a heavy sack.

I don't know why the wedges of cheese wouldn't go any further. I zipped up the teddy bear and followed the cow. It was walking slowly, because of the debris, and also because the street was too narrow for it. The cow was really fat, but it kept on walking. As it moved its fat body brushed against the walls of the buildings on either side. Sometimes a plant would fall down and get trampled on the ground and the cow would stop, lower its head and eat it. There were other plants that had been trampled and buried under the rubble but the cow didn't notice those ones. It only ate the plants that fell as a result of its body rubbing along the walls of the buildings.

I wanted to follow the cow to find out where it would go, but I was worried about losing track of the cinema, so I retraced my steps. Along the way I tried to get some of the plants out from under the rubble but the stones were heavy and I could shift them only a fraction of an inch. I really wanted to feed the dead plants to the cow, because I thought the cow might be frightened. Perhaps she only ate the plants that fell because it was easier and it meant she didn't have to stop for long.

But this cow wasn't like those cows that fall off trucks or escape from their farm the night before they are due to be slaughtered and hide in a school classroom with tears in their black eyes and their hearts beating rapidly. It was very different from any cow anyone might ever have heard of. It had belonged to a soldier and he kept looking for her. On the way to the cinema he stopped me and asked me if I had seen a cow in the area. I knew from his uniform that he was one of the soldiers who were the reason we had taken shelter in the cinema. So when he started talking to me, I was frightened and I almost started crying. But he said he wouldn't harm me if I showed him where the cow was. I told him I hadn't seen a cow in the area. I felt I was telling the truth, the whole truth, and that I really hadn't seen a cow anywhere. He also asked me about the teddy bear and I told him it was for food and had wedges of cheese in it. But he wasn't interested. He didn't ask me to unzip the teddy to make sure. There was a pistol on his hip.

The soldier told me he had brought the cow from his home far away and that when they enlisted him he couldn't possibly part with his cow, so he had brought her along with him. He loved her very much. He said the cow sat with him in the tank. He got it into the tank without the officers knowing. But he had lost it a few days earlier. His tank had been ambushed and his arm was wounded and he lost consciousness. When he came round, he asked about the cow and they thought he was hallucinating. They gave him an injection to make him sleep. He said he spent a week being injected with tranquillizers, whether he asked about the cow or not. Then they sent him back to the army. But how the cow managed to clamber out of the tank, he didn't know. He was talking and I was listening. He said he had been going up to the flats where people were living. He would knock on a door and when the people opened it, he would ask them, 'Are there any terrorists here?' But he wasn't interested in 'terrorists', only in his cow. He didn't go into the flats, but from the doorway he would take a peek inside to see if she was there or not. He knew the sound of her voice well and could tell it apart from other cows'. His cow couldn't stand strangers, so she would definitely moo as soon as she saw her soldier friend.

When the soldier finished speaking, I left. I said, 'I haven't seen your cow,' and walked away. He walked off in another direction, resuming his search for the cow. Before I got back to the cinema, I decided I would kill the cow when I next saw her; if I couldn't kill her, I would have to hurt her, so that he couldn't possibly put her back in the tank. I was certain for some reason that she would come through the projection room the next morning, and that's exactly what happened.

And I ended up walking after her again.

The cow followed the same path. This time I was determined to get to the buildings before her. I ran as fast as I could, holding the teddy bear in my hand. It started swinging in the air slowly because its stomach was stuffed with wedges of cheese. I overtook the cow and stopped at the first building. I took out a piece of cheese and filled the cracks in the wall of the building with it. I did the same thing with every building I came to. When the cow's body rubbed against the buildings, no plants now fell off, and so the cow would die of hunger. I kept up with the cow for three days, reaching the buildings first and filling the cracks with cheese. The cow often changed course and went to other buildings, but I would get there first and I would never give her a chance to rub any plants off the walls. The cow didn't eat anything for three days straight and then it collapsed on the ground from hunger. Because it was a cow and not a cat, it wouldn't lick the cheese off the walls as a cat might do.

The cow was half-dead and I was exhausted too. With a sense of relief I stopped to look at her. I even kicked her. But the kick didn't hurt her at all. Over the previous few days I'd done a lot – I'd spent most of the time filling the cracks with cheese and I hadn't eaten a single piece. I hadn't eaten anything all the days I'd been working, because I needed to use all the wedges. My only rest was when I slept on the cinema seat facing the projection room. I didn't sit in any other chair, because it was the only seat facing the projection room and from it I could see the cow passing in the morning.

The cow started mooing as it lay on the ground. I was frightened the soldier might hear it mooing and come and arrest me. Fortunately the mooing was faint because her body was so weak. I had to find some way to torment the cow without the soldier detecting it if he found her.

Among the rubble I found four footballs. They were all punctured. I gathered them together and went over to the cow. When she saw me approaching with the balls she tried to get up. She was frightened – very frightened. She took a few steps but she soon collapsed on the ground panting. I seized the opportunity and slipped a piece of rubber football into her mouth. The cow rejected it at first, but she was so hungry she started to chew the piece of rubber. Then she swallowed it.

In the end the cow ate all four footballs. But instead of the cow suffering and having diarrhoea, for example, or stomach cramps, her body fattened up and her health improved. I tried other things: pieces of broken china, old fruit, mouldy bread, a shoe lace, the buckle of a school satchel, a key ring – everything except photographs and cassettes. The cow ate them without complaining. She had put on weight and had recovered her vigour. But her eyes were sad. I avoided looking at her so that I wouldn't cry. She was now strangely swollen and her coat was standing on end. She looked rather like a giant white hedgehog with black spots. She began looking for anything to eat. The next day I saw her eating some halva, some cake and some pastries full of cream.

On the final day the cow came as usual in the morning. She walked through the projection room, but slowly. She was bigger than ever before, and she weighed more than her legs could bear. She was also dirty and bruised. Maybe she had stumbled on the way or some-body had fallen on her from the ruined buildings around the cinema, the ones where I had filled the cracks with cheese. Recently flies had started eating the cheese and maybe that had affected the strength of those buildings. I was sitting on the same seat in the cinema, and everything was still around me. There was no one there but me. Neither my mother nor my sister nor the others. The cow's eyes looked at me through the opening in the projection room, but this time she didn't go anywhere. She couldn't leave the projection room. Instead of taking a step forward, she sat down where she was. I got up from my seat in the cinema and went into the projection room. I wanted the cow to leave, to go walking as she did every day. But she just sat there. I aimed a few kicks at her, but she didn't groan or moo. I tried to push her with both hands but my pushes were very feeble and ineffective. I stepped back a little and looked at her. Then I went back to the auditorium and sat in my seat watching the cow. I knew she wouldn't leave. Now the cow was blocking the sunlight that usually came into the auditorium in the morning through the hole in the wall of the projection room. Now the auditorium was completely dark, just like it was when all the lights went out. Just like it was when the film was about to begin.

Biscuits

MY MOTHER WAS SITTING QUIETLY IN THE BACK seat. I was telling my wife a joke and driving the car. We were on our way to the care home, taking my mother back after her day out with us. My mother stays at the care home six days a week. Alzheimer's. The car was travelling at fifty miles an hour. This is not just a detail. I never found out whether my wife got the joke or not, since she didn't have a chance to laugh. Just as I finished telling the joke, we saw an old man crossing the motorway on the other side. When you're travelling at high speed, sudden death looks like it's happening in slow motion.

I stopped the car, of course, like a number of other people, and with my wife's help I got my mother out of the car and left her to watch the scene from behind the concrete barrier. The old man was truly amazing. He was hopping nimbly between the vehicles, avoiding one car, dodging and weaving, whirling around, spinning like a wheel, doing the splits and throwing feeble punches. I kept my mother and my wife at a safe distance so that the old man wouldn't touch us with his boxing gloves and turn us into biscuits. The old man's gloves grew bigger and bigger whenever he touched the side of a car and turned it into a biscuit. My wife tried to say something to the old man, but I nudged her with my elbow and she realized she should keep silent. As for my mother, her eyes drank in the whole scene, especially when I started describing it to her in precise detail, with the enthusiasm of a sports commentator: 'He's touching the side of a car and turning it into a biscuit.'

The old man didn't look anxious. He stepped out into the motorway between the speeding cars, then took off his white hat and wrapped it around his fist like a boxing glove. He didn't want to punch the cars, just to touch them. The speeding cars tried to avoid him, but they didn't succeed. Every car he touched turned into a giant biscuit. Since they were going so fast, they overturned and crumbled into pieces by the side of the road. The scene was riveting to watch as the first three groups of cars passed. Soon there was a giant pile of biscuit crumbs on the side of the road.

Later, on the way to the care home, my wife said with a smile that she would have liked to ask the old man just one question. I didn't comment. We reached the door of the care home. I got my mother out of the car and, as I handed her over to a beautiful nurse, I whispered in her ear, 'Mum, tell the nice lady the story about the old man.' And Mother did then launch into a monologue about the biscuits as she went off with the nurse. I heard the latter saying, 'And what else happened?' My mother fell silent because she could no longer remember, and the nurse then suggested, 'How about giving you an injection to help you remember the rest of the story?'

This is what I usually do with my mother: I present her with a story once a week. Last week we were alone – my wife wasn't with us. I stopped the car in front of a biscuit seller. He's a boy who carries on his back an enormous canvas bag full of giant biscuits that he sells by the kilo. They're the kind of biscuits used for making desserts at home. He targets cars with elderly women, confident they are mothers.

He came up to the car window, saying to my mother, 'Madam, would you like some biscuits? Take one and give me whatever you like for it.' But my mother didn't answer. She didn't know for a moment what the boy was talking about. 'Mum,' I said. 'Biscuits – you know what biscuits are, don't you?' But she didn't answer. I asked the boy to get a biscuit out of his bag and show it to her. 'It's a massive biscuit, isn't it, Mum?' I said. My mother smiled at the sight of the giant biscuit. 'That one's half the size of the bonnet of the Renault 5 that I'm driving,' I said. Then I added that the boy had other biscuits, some of them the size of tiles and some as big as a classroom blackboard.

Mother could no longer make the delicious desserts she had been so good at making during the war. Baking a cake requires intense concentration and in some cases determination as well. My mother would carry on in the midst of bombing raids and when the neighbours and their children were shouting. She'd tell us to go down to the shelter with Father while she stayed in the kitchen. She'd join us only when her cake was ready, and her cakes always had biscuits as the main ingredient, because it was cheaper than filling them with chocolate, cream or fruit. My father loved cake with biscuits.

In the care home my mother would sometimes throw a tantrum and tell her doctor that it was me who made up all these stories. The doctor summoned me several times to ask me whether what she said was true. I denied it of course. I'd say that my mother had Alzheimer's and that's all there was to it. It was Alzheimer's that made her confused and led to these accusations. She said, 'The old man was dead and covered in blood. He'd made a desperate attempt to block the motorway, but a car ran him over. I didn't see any biscuits.' But she'd add that she wasn't certain about this, and then she'd collapse, so they would give her an injection to tranquillize her.

I know my mother doesn't have Alzheimer's. My mother also knows that. And maybe the doctor does too. But I pay the care-home bills regularly, including those for the Alzheimer's treatment. Not so that my mother will stay in the care home, but to try to make sure she goes on believing in the biscuit story. I visit my mother every Wednesday as well as at the weekend. I stay with her for an hour or an hour and a half. My mother doesn't say anything when I tell her that the old man that I showed her is still on the motorway. 'He has his white gloves on and he's touching the cars. Some of the drivers have tried to crash into him, including a soldier in an army jeep. All of them have ended up as biscuits. So far no one's been able to get him off the motorway. And the old man is just as you saw him the first time, Mum. He darts between the cars. He hops around on one leg. He spares one car. He dodges and weaves. He spins around. They tried using tranquillizer darts on him, but he dodged them all. Warning shots weren't any use either. The sight of the old man is now so commonplace that people no longer stop on the side of the road to watch – except for tourists, who take pictures or videos of the old man on their phones. There were three big fire engines on the side of the motorway today. Whenever the old man turns a car into a biscuit, the firemen immediately spray the biscuit with their hoses to soak it and free the people inside.' Then my mother asked, 'Don't you think that the old man who turns cars into biscuits looks like your father?' My mother is talking about my father, though there has been no trace of him for more than twenty years, ever since he packed his bags at the end of the war, claiming he was going off for some sporting event. My mother still goes to the window every day and curses him out loud, so much so that it's annoying for the neighbours and embarrassing for me.

Every weekend my wife and I go past the old man on the motorway. My mother sits in the back of the car. There comes a moment when I watch my mother in the rear-view mirror, whispering, 'The old man's coming closer now, to touch our car.' At that point my wife automatically exclaims, 'Hey, old man, now are you satisfied?' My mother is now convinced that whenever the old man hears this, he freezes, which gives us a chance to escape. Sometimes a police patrol car draws alongside us and one of the policemen asks us why we've stopped in the middle of the motorway, and my wife and I have an argument. I don't approve of revealing any details of this story to anyone except my mother, and whenever it's her day out I do everything I can to make her think we're going to bake a cake in the kitchen.

A Joke

I'M TRYING TO MAKE UP A JOKE, A COMPLETELY new joke. I don't have ready-made jokes in my head and I don't remember any details of the few jokes I've heard. So I'm trying to sketch out the scenario for a joke in my head. I look around me. There's nothing I can use in my joke except for my parents. They're not my real parents. They're my adoptive parents, and their son has gone out to beg. He might not be their real son – he too might be adopted. Some people say he's my brother, but I don't believe it, although there is a resemblance. Sometimes I feel sorry for him, because he has only one arm. But with it he can beg, whereas I can't.

He's the only breadwinner in the household, because my adoptive parents are old. I'm still young, they say. None the less, my health problem prevents me from begging or working. I'm too embarrassed to tell anyone about it. It might be simple for you. It might not be worth mentioning. What kind of work can a young man like me do when he has to urinate every quarter of an hour? How does that happen? I don't know. Although I don't drink much water, I always need to urinate, even when I'm asleep. For a time, I would wet my bed – the whole bed. Or, if I happened to be sleeping in the court-yard, where there were piles of rubbish, I would soak the paper I was sleeping on. My parents didn't mind me sleeping there, and I don't see anything wrong with someone sleeping in their own rubbish; what's wrong is to sleep in the middle of other people's rubbish. But I no longer do that, because I'm a year or two older. When you grow up, you think more and you find ways to avoid a particular problem. So now I wear nappies and I can sleep wherever I like.

Sometimes I sleep on the sofa and imagine that the television is on and that I'm watching all the channels at once. I don't know how to do that, but there must be a way to see all the channels at the same time. Then my brother comes back from work, takes the bar of soap out of my hand and says, 'This is not a remote control,' slowly and in a loud voice, like this: 'THIS . . . IS . . . NOT . . . A . . . REMOTE . . . CONTROL.' Then he carries me to the bedroom. When I'm asleep, I can only walk with someone else's legs.

We share the bedroom, him and me. During the day,

we use it as a kitchen, while the old people are asleep in the next room. In the winter I used to sleep in the courtyard, between the piles of rubbish. It was warmer like that. With his one arm my brother makes me a mat out of newspapers. He collects the newspapers during the day from the nearby shops, the hairdressing salons, the coffee shops and the supermarkets. Every day my brother begs in a different street – for the novelty value. A new beggar attracts attention. And every day I try to think of a joke to tell him, because I don't have any other way to thank him. I say, 'One day I'm going to make up a long, beautiful joke for you that will make you laugh for two days straight – you won't stop laughing, even for a minute.' He shakes his head. I don't remember seeing my brother laugh. Not since he caught sight of himself in the glass door of a large building and he saw that he had an arm and a half instead of two arms. My parents say he came out of my mother's belly like that.

I know my new joke won't turn my brother into a happy beggar. But I want it to be powerful enough to be included in my CV and to stand the test of time. I want my brother to laugh non-stop for two whole days so that he can't go to work – like any beggar, he wouldn't collect a single penny if he stood on the pavement with his one arm stretched out, chuckling with laughter. The food in the house will run out, because we won't have money to last two days, and, besides, when you laugh a lot you get hungry.

My mother hides the nappies that are left and throws the mop at me, and I have to clean up my urine, which has soaked my clothes, the toilet seat, the floor, the bed, and the courtyard. Sometimes I slip, and sometimes I wet myself while cleaning up the previous round, while my brother laughs, slapping his forehead with the muscles of his one arm and saying with difficulty, 'It's no use, man, no use.'

The Angel of Death

I DON'T HAVE A SENSE OF HUMOUR, TO BE HONEST, and I don't understand why people smile. You'll usually find me scowling. I don't look at faces when I'm walking along and I don't say hello to anyone. That's because people don't let me say hello to them when I'm scowling. You're supposed to smile whenever you raise your hand or nod your head to greet someone, whether in the morning or the afternoon, even if you meet someone in a dark alley. This is exhausting in itself. But if you greet someone without smiling, they'll be hostile and, I assure you, they'll look in the other direction the next time. I've thought about this subject at length, and because every time I greet someone, it costs me a smile that I'm not really able to produce, I prefer not to greet them in the first place. That doesn't mean I wouldn't like to greet people. Not at all. I just can't smile. Find me a solution. If I said hello to someone with my head bowed,

97

they'd think I wasn't paying enough attention or there was something wrong with me, that I had something to be ashamed of, or that I'd suffered some setback or was the victim of some serious mishap. And so, in order to avoid all the confusion I might cause to others, I've decided not to look at anyone when I'm walking along. Not to look up at all.

I've been doing this for forty-four years, ever since my ninth birthday. I stood in front of my father and said, 'From now on I'm not going to smile at anyone.' My father laughed and didn't take me seriously. When a boy of nine tells you he's not going to smile from now on, you don't believe him, of course. No one in this world can stop themselves from smiling altogether. You'd think it was just something the child said on the spur of the moment. But that wasn't the case with me.

My father told my mother, who gave me a big hug and said some playful words of the kind that make children laugh. But I didn't smile. That was the first time I acted on my decision not to smile. 'Decision' isn't really the right word, though. It would be better to call it a 'theme'. So that was the first time I put into effect my no-smiling theme: in my mother's arms.

I now have the courage to say it was a good start. When you're in your mother's tender arms and you refuse to smile, it means you have the self-confidence not to smile at the whole world. I didn't mean to offend my mother, or my father. But they were crestfallen and they started to argue. My first thought was that if I smiled, an ambulance would come and take me away. This was just a feeling and I couldn't really explain it. I had decided not to smile and that was that. When some child asked me, I would say, 'If I smile, an ambulance will come and take me away,' and they would burst out laughing. Then my father died. And then it wasn't long before my mother also joined the ranks of the dead.

My parents died without seeing me smile. I was a teenager by then. I remember that on her deathbed my mother begged me to smile. As she was breathing her last, she said, 'Let me see you smile.' But that was the last thing that was going to happen. At that moment, more than ever, I couldn't smile. It's true that I didn't try, because I simply couldn't in those circumstances; deep down, I knew it was impossible. I would have liked to borrow a smile from the face of some neighbour. I imagined knocking on their door; they would open it with a smile and I would snatch the smile off their face, slap it on my face and rush back to my mother. What could I say to her? I felt powerless and I started to sob. The neighbours hurried over and gathered in the room. There were about twenty people around the bed. They started mumbling prayers meant to help my mother's soul on its way as it left her body. But my mother paid no attention to any of them. She mustered the last of her strength and managed to say, 'Please, just one smile.' But I couldn't do it. My face was as rigid as a jam sandwich left over from yesterday. Since my problem was well known to everyone, the neighbours set their minds to helping me. They immediately stopped reciting prayers and started telling jokes they remembered. I was bombarded with dozens of jokes, one after the other, including some dirty ones. That was how the well-intentioned neighbours tried to bring a smile to my face. I leave you to imagine the scene – my mother about to die, asking me for a smile, the neighbours telling jokes around the bed, and me unable to smile. A few minutes later my mother did die and I got into an argument with the neighbours and threw them out of the room. I couldn't control myself. I behaved like a maniac.

Days later I visited a psychiatrist, who took extensive notes and wrote me a prescription. After a few sessions he sent me away and said he would contact me, and I went home. The doctor still hasn't contacted me and I haven't heard anything from him. This happened a long time ago. There are plenty of details but I no longer remember them. Now I feel that I owe my mother a smile but I will never be able to repay the debt.

Long after my mother died I was still living in the

same house. I didn't feel I was any different from other people. My neighbours had grown used to me as a man who didn't smile or say hello to anyone. And by now I walked with a pronounced stoop that even animals noticed.

I didn't tell you what drove the psychiatrist to throw me out of his clinic. When he put his stethoscope to my chest, he didn't hear a heartbeart. He heard, 'Ha, ha, ha.'

'What the fuck kind of game are you playing with me?' he said angrily. That led to an argument, I ended up at home thinking about it, and he never called.

As time passed and I grew old, my back became as solid as the back of an old rhinoceros. My head was now level with my waist, so that I looked like this: ٦. I looked as if I was staring at the ground as I walked, as if someone had told me off. But that's not how it was in fact. You won't believe what I'm going to say. My back had become as strong as a plank of wood and it had grown broad and flat, so I found myself a job, as a birthday porter. I would stand rooted to the spot and carry children's birthday parties on my back. A session would sometimes last three hours and sometimes four. It would be wrong to call it a session. More properly it was a 'standing' or a 'station'. I made sure I arrived on time and soon my back would be covered in children. They would climb up, shouting excitedly. The child, the friends he or she'd invited, his mother and father and siblings would gather together to celebrate the child's birthday, but I couldn't see anything. I could just hear the children's voices coming from above. And their giggles. While I was staring at the floor. Pretty much like a portable shelf. Or a podium. If I were asked, I'd prefer the term *shelf. Podium* would be an exaggeration. And wherever the child's parents chose to hold a birthday party, I would go.

You might see me standing in a park, on the beach, or even in a school playground. My appearance did provoke some strange looks. Sometimes people would flock to see me, stare and take pictures. But I didn't care. I earned a reasonable fee. Then, when everyone had left, I went back home. I did face one problem, and that was how to wash my back, which was as solid as a piece of concrete, and which was bare when the kids climbed up. You know how children's birthday parties can get very messy. So I had to sluice my back well. But the neighbours helped me. They took me to the garage and washed me with the fine spray from a hose. My massive body didn't bother them. They were nice – they cared about my feelings and didn't smile, share jokes or tell funny stories while they were washing me. But from my house later I could hear them roaring with laughter. Maybe they were making fun of me.

The joyful voices of the children should cheer me up and make me want to smile. But that doesn't happen in my case. Even when a child hands me a sweet before climbing up onto my back, I don't smile. I say, 'Thank you,' but the child thinks I'm not excited about their birthday, because I seem to be scowling.

I would like to say that there's a difference between scowling and not smiling. But how can you convince a child of that? If you don't smile at a child on their birthday, they'll be confused. And then the child's mother steps in to tell me off. And then I have to make an effort to convince the child that I'm not scowling and that it's nothing personal. If I didn't do that, I wouldn't get my fee. 'I'm not frowning,' I tell the child. And from on top of me, the child replies, 'Well if you're not frowning, why aren't you smiling?'

'I just don't know how to smile,' I reply.

The other children on my back soon join in and throw cake at me, trying to hit my face. And then the party's over.

This has happened at more than four parties, which was enough to persuade me to change my job. I remember that on one occasion I told the children, 'If I smile, my back will shake and the whole lot of you will fall off.' Their reaction was to cling onto my back, using their horribly sharp little fingernails, and ask me to smile. That hurt. One of the children said, 'Smile and we won't fall off.' But I didn't smile of course. Even if there hadn't been the misunderstanding with the children, I would have had to stop carrying them at birthday parties anyway. That was because my back bent further and further forwards, until it was no longer horizontal. On several occasions pigeons would try to shelter from the rain underneath me and I had to run and hide from them. And then some homeless old people gathered around me while I was urinating in an alley and started to examine me – they thought that I was a slide. Some of them even tried to slide down me. I didn't move an inch until I'd finished urinating. I picked myself up slowly and left. And what did those vagrants do? They burst out laughing of course. I've no idea why an old man would think of sliding down a slide. The very thought troubles me. I felt humiliated, and the next day I found myself stalking an old vagrant and pouncing on him.

The poor man freaked out. He pissed in his pants. All he had to defend himself with was a half-litre can of beer – he started spraying me with it and screaming. He was frightened by the idea that a slide was attacking him. I dragged him bodily to the garage and washed the urine off him with the hose the neighbours use to wash me. The same hose. My neighbours are bastards, I know that. That's my final judgment on them. I withdraw what

I said about them before. I didn't tell you that they place bets on who can make me giggle when they're washing me. They poke me in the ribs, as if I were their dumb whore. They want me to laugh without me noticing that they're tickling me.

One of the neighbours came out of his bedroom and stood on the balcony while I was washing the homeless man and said, 'Tickle him until he laughs.' I didn't know how to answer him. But any response from me would have seemed rude. The bastard just stood on the balcony, laughing, before turning back into his house. Meanwhile the old man I was hosing down was shivering as I washed him. He was one of a group of men who lived under a bridge that had acquired a bad reputation in the war. 'Are you the angel of death?' he asked me, trembling.

'Do you think the angel of death will wash you with a hosepipe in a garage before he seizes your soul?' I said, and he started to laugh. I didn't like him laughing, since I hadn't intended to make a joke. For a start, I don't have a sense of humour, I'm not trying to develop one, and I don't want to be good at making up jokes. So I told him, 'I am in fact the angel of death, but before I seize your soul you have to tell me what makes an old man think of sliding down a slide.' Then I pointed the hose up in the air, blocked the end with my thumb, and asked him to give me an answer before the jet of water I was about to release came back down and hit the floor. But the old man didn't give me an answer. Why? Because his heart had stopped. Before the jet of water hit the floor, he had breathed his last in the garage. That must have been because the real angel of death was in the neighbourhood. I won't deny that I freaked out. I'd never had a chance to kill anyone before, so I didn't know how to behave when I did. I immediately tried to drag the old man's body back to the bridge, but the police surrounded me. Of course! When you get in a state, your bastard neighbours take the chance to denounce you. But the old man didn't have any identity papers on him, so they released me. That's all. I want to add one observation, and that is that my life has totally changed. I now live in a completely different way. I enjoy everyone's respect, including that of my bastard neighbours. Even if they send me to prison, I'll be able to survive among the most hardened and infamous criminals. Because, although I've spent most of my life unable to smile, I now know that I'm a man who can kill people with a joke.

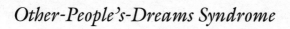

Other-People's-Dreams Syndrome

WHEN HOSSAM DREAMS, HE ISN'T THE MAIN character in the dream. In fact he may not even be a character at all. Every time he's in a dream it feels like he's been given a new soul and a new life, but it's always in a context of marginal importance. 'Why does this happen to me?' he asked me one day, while I was paying bail to get him out of detention.

As soon as he shuts his eyes, he imagines himself in a changing room in someone else's dream. He takes off his old personality and puts on a new one, and then he's summoned to take his place in the dream. His name changes from one dream to the next. It depends on what he's going to do. Very often he doesn't have a name at all. And because he's so insignificant in the dreams he finds himself in, it may be that no one addresses him directly. As soon as Hossam hears one of the cast members in the dream shouting something like, 'Bring the pencil sharpener,' or, 'Where's the dog?' or, 'Give the hero the ashtray,' he gets himself ready, because that's what Hossam's going to be – the pencil sharpener, the dog or the ashtray. He's never been the hero – unless a pencil sharpener, a dog or an ashtray can play the star role in some dream.

His dreams usually start in the same way, in a changing room. 'It's a noisy place. It's like they're filming the dream, as in the movies,' he says. 'Every dream has someone in charge, like the director of a film.' His function is to manage the dream; he has the exclusive right to do so – because he's the man who dreams. You'll find him stroking his dog, scratching his balls, or lecherously kissing a girl who wants to be someone else. In his other hand he holds a pair of binoculars to monitor the progress of the dream. Hossam has even seen himself as the girl the director is kissing. He said he was annoyed, but he kissed the man and even let the director fondle his bottom. In a whisper, after I promised on my honour I wouldn't tell anyone, he said, 'I was a girl in the dream. Imagine. Have you ever dreamt you're a girl? I have. Another annoying thing about it was that I was a girl who would do anything to be a star, a wannabe girl. That was bad enough, but the kissing made it worse.' Then there are the mistakes that the characters in the dream sometimes make, which means they have to redo the whole dream. It doesn't happen on the same night but on the following night, and without Hossam knowing about it. 'That's cheating, don't you think? To go to sleep and find you're repeating the same dream,' he tells me.

In one six-dream sequence he saw himself laid out on a trolley in hospital. 'That was frightening. There were nurses pushing me along the corridor but I didn't know where I was going. I might have been going down to the mortuary or heading for intensive care. From the number of nurses around me, I gathered I was in a critical condition.' Even so, Hossam wasn't the main character in this dream. In every version of the dream his trolley went past a man shouting, 'No, no, no,' and this man was the main character in the dream, although all he said was 'no'.

'His shouting was annoying and unpleasant. I even tried to give him the finger, regardless of whatever tragedy he was going through, but apparently that wasn't allowed. I tried to wake up but I couldn't. He was the focal point of the dream, and I was just part of the décor. You know how in a dream you see people in the distance – in the background? I'm always in the background of other people's dreams.' It seems the dreamer wasn't satisfied with his dream. He wanted his dream to be perfect from a dramatic point of view. So he kept revising it in his head for six days straight.

'My God! That's like having to sit through a trial,' I joked. He said he didn't care, trial or no trial, but he had to put a stop to it. 'Why all these tricks? I've never done anyone any harm.'

'Sure, not until you started seeing yourself in other people's dreams,' I said.

Hossam is right to object. Usually he's extremely polite. For him, politeness is a choice, a defence, like the shell of a snail. It's the most effective way to avoid people and keep your interactions superficial. 'Then you can peel yourself away from them whenever you want, without them feeling any pain' – that's his philosophy.

Hossam lived in a small room, by himself. He shared the shower with neighbours. The shower was outside his room. He only took a shower after checking that everyone else had had a shower before him. Sometime he waited till late at night. And he had only one friend, which was me. And I loved his politeness.

In one of the dreams, he found himself in a romantic relationship with a girl. I don't know if his politeness had anything to do with it. 'We started the relationship quickly. Faster than you can imagine. Within minutes we were lovers. I ended up kissing her in her car. On the motorway. She was the one driving. But an old man came up alongside us and started cursing and making obscene gestures with his hands. Then he gave up and overtook us. A few minutes later we found ourselves stuck in a traffic jam, and we started kissing like crazy and the other drivers were looking at us. We took no notice. I even squeezed her left breast. But the dirty old man reappeared, parked close to a traffic policeman. He had reported us, and we were wanted for offending public morals. As soon as we approached, he pointed at us and started cursing. The policeman stopped us and started preaching a sermon, more like a priest than a policeman. I bowed my head in embarrassment and the girl started crying.' The next morning, when Hossam woke up, he still felt guilty. He got dressed and headed straight to a flower shop. He bought a bunch of flowers and started to draft a message apologizing to the girl, whom he saw every day. She lived near the travel agency where he worked. The thing about her that had caught his attention was the fact that she wore white rubber boots.

The flowers he was carrying were also white. 'She must love white,' he said. She might even stick one of them in her boot.

Hossam went up to the girl, said, 'I apologize,' and offered her the flowers. The girl was surprised, or maybe she pretended to be surprised. When she asked him why he was apologizing, he said, 'Didn't you dream about me last night?'

'Sorry? Why would I dream about you? Do I even know you?'

'No, but you dreamed about me,' he replied.

Then Hossam started to get agitated and more aggressive. Passers-by gathered around him. It was like a scene from *Candid Camera*. People were smiling and looking at the buildings to find the hidden camera. 'This girl dreamed about me last night,' said Hossam. 'I'm sure of it. Ask her. It was just a few hours ago and now she's trying to pretend I'm nothing to do with her. What nonsense!' But the girl wasn't lying. She really didn't recognize him.

'Liar! Liar!' Hossam started shouting. Then he threw the flowers on the ground and trampled on them. 'I hope your flowers burn in hell,' he said.

He ended up in the police station and almost lost his job.

I fully agree that Hossam wasn't responsible for his problems.

Sometimes he dreamed that he was a pressing human need. I remember him telling me how he saw himself in a dream as a pair of glasses hanging on the branch of a tree. The glasses belonged to a little boy who was crying beneath the tree. The little boy was the main character, since he was sitting in the dream director's chair. But he didn't do anything. The boy was lazy. Very lazy, in fact, because the branch wasn't that high. 'What was he waiting for? For an earthquake to happen and the glasses to fall and save the situation?'

Hossam's absolutely worst dream was when he saw himself as a piece of dog shit on the pavement. He couldn't do anything about it. 'I couldn't jump off somewhere or even crawl. I was firmly stuck to the ground. And I was sweating. I must have been a fresh piece of shit, a piece of shit that had just come out. But from where I was, I couldn't see a dog nearby. I thought I would never get out of this dream and would spend the rest of my life as a piece of shit on the pavement. A few minutes later war broke out, and it was a vicious war, with RPGs and machine guns. There was an invasion, with armed men taking up their positions.'

While he was looking for the dream director, who wasn't visible anywhere, Hossam saw an army boot, which landed on him and lifted him up off the pavement. 'Hey, man, imagine you're the piece of shit that's stuck to the boot of a gunman during what appears to be an attack. While his comrades move forward according to the plan, the gunman stops and tries to get you off his boot because the smell's interfering with his concentration. He rubs you against the pavement and starts cursing the guts that produced you. Moments later he realizes that he's a target. No one's covering him and his comrades have moved ahead, either because the smell is so strong or for strategic reasons determined by how long the attack is expected to last. Then he starts shooting to protect himself. He's scraping his boot to get the shit off and firing his rifle at the same time. At random, of course. Except he took a bullet or two in his leg, and then in his hip. Blood flowed, soaked his combat trousers, ran down into his boot and then touched me. Because of the blood, I fell off the boot, but I was still wet with that gunman's blood.'

Not all his dreams were frightening. Once he saw himself as a kiss. Hossam wasn't the lips that shared the kiss. 'I was the kiss itself. I don't know how to explain that. I was just a feeling in the dream.'

The people who took on the role of film director in his dreams might be Hossam's neighbours, or sometimes members of his family. Even his former wife. I had spoken to some of them at the police station or the hospital. They assured me that, to their surprise, what Hossam said about their dreams was one hundred per cent true. Some people were going to file a complaint against Hossam in court – they didn't want Hossam holding them responsible for their dreams.

All Hossam could do was wait for the main character in his dream to wake up and open their eyes. At that point Hossam would wake up too, shaking off the blanket irritably and cursing the person in whose dream he'd found himself. He would put on his dressing gown and his sandals and, straight out of bed, without washing or even combing his hair, he'd head over to his neighbour's. He'd knock on the door. The neighbour was caught off guard when Hossam jumped in with his question: 'Can you tell me what you dreamed about last night?'

Hossam wasn't on close terms with any of his neighbours. His relationship with them was distant. So it was odd for him to ask them directly about their dream when he had never had a proper conversation with them. They wouldn't talk about their dream, so Hossam told them his version. They were surprised. Hossam took advantage of their surprise to lay into them with his fists, shouting, 'This is a violation of privacy. This is a violation of privacy.' Sometimes he would take the day off work and go by bus to settle a score with some dreamer.

He tried all kinds of ways to avoid other people's dreams, but none of them worked. In the end he joined a shooting club, in the hope that he might transfer his new skills to other people's dreams and kill them by mistake. 'Mistakes do happen, even in dreams, don't they?' he said.

Although he didn't yet have a gun licence, he managed to buy a Colt revolver and he carried it around with him wherever he went, to the supermarket or to work. Even when he went to bed, he stuffed it behind his back in the hope that it would go into his dream with him. 'Do you sleep with the revolver on your hip?' I asked him. When he said yes, I was dismayed. I was worried he might use it against one of the people he dreamed about.

When he couldn't recognize the person in whose dream he was, he'd call me in a nervous state. He started having suspicions about everyone, including me. 'Why isn't the dreamer someone I know? Why not you, for example?'

'Me?' I said in a panic, glancing at the glint of the silver revolver. 'Definitely not. Not me. Upon my honour. I've never seen you in any of my dreams. What's come over you? Aren't we friends?'

In his room you could find rough sketches of the people who'd dreamed about Hossam and whom he'd never seen in real life. He became obsessed with hunting them down, even if it took him the rest of his life. 'Why do people you don't know, that you've never seen, drag you into their dreams? What do they want from you?' he asked.

His mental state was deteriorating and I couldn't do anything to help him. It bothered me. I became frightened of him. What if Hossam appeared in a minor role in one of my dreams, without me being able to tell? I knew he was counting on me to give him the main role in one of my dreams. At least in one dream. But he never said that overtly.

I avoided seeing him or keeping in touch with him. I didn't want to risk it. What if I had dreamed about him and I couldn't remember? And when I mistreated something in a dream, I worried that the thing might in fact be Hossam. I was tense, and he would ask me enthusiastically, 'So tell me, are you suffering from other-people's-dreams syndrome too?'

'No. Not yet,' I said.

Then the end came when he found himself in a dream about a boy with a mental disability. He was the son of some neighbours, an old couple who hadn't had any other children. His mind had stopped developing when he was three years old. Now he was as old as an adult but he had the mind of a child. His parents grew older. Hossam had never imagined he would end up in this boy's dream, but that's what happened.

The boy was sitting in the dream director's chair. He was giving instructions, none of which Hossam understood, but he did allow Hossam to bring his revolver with him. Hossam was chasing his ex-wife in front of the boy. His wife hadn't had any children. Hossam fired at her but didn't hit her. What happened was that the bullet hit the boy by mistake, near his waist. Hossam woke up in a panic and called me immediately. 'I've shot the disabled boy and killed him,' he said, 'but it happened by accident.' He was speaking as though this had really happened. I calmed him down and we agreed to meet for a coffee in a cafe. I waited for Hossam for about thirty minutes before he finally came. It wasn't his practice to be late. On the contrary, after every bad dream he'd had, I'd usually find that he had beaten me to the coffee shop and was sitting there nervously. When he finally arrived, his face had turned yellow, as if someone had urinated on him. 'What's up now?' I asked him, as if I were asking a spoiled child. 'The boy really has died. I heard his parents weeping. He woke up with horrible pains in his kidneys and was groaning loudly, and the parents, who move slowly because of their age, couldn't do anything for him. He soon died. He died because I shot him. In the dream the bullet lodged near his waist.'

I tried to convince him that this was impossible. A bullet he had fired in a dream couldn't lead to the boy really dying. Then he handed himself in at the police station, but they didn't take a statement from him. Instead, they referred him to a hospital that specializes in mental and nervous disorders. I had to escort him and sign the papers for his admission and tell them how long he planned to stay.

In the hospital Hossam became good friends with

the other inmates. They were always hovering around him and he no longer complained about the dreams. In fact he liked the mental patients' dreams. Then he asked me to smuggle in the Colt revolver for him. 'Impossible,' I said. 'Are you planning to commit a crime?'

'No. For days I've been dreaming about myself. About me. I found myself as a child, a little child dreaming about me. Do you get what I mean? I'm two people in the dream – the child I was in the past and the grown-up man you're talking to now. I don't know which of the two is the extra in the life of the other, the adult or the child. But what's certain is that it's the child that's dreaming, and not me.'

'And what do you plan to do with the revolver?' I asked him.

'I'm going to shoot the boy dead. Just as I did with the son of the old couple. And since the boy will die, he won't wake up, which means that I won't leave the dream. I'll supervise his funeral in the dream.'

'That's enough, Hossam. Enough. You have to get out of this vicious circle, or whatever you call it. Do you think I believe you? I'm fed up.' That was the last thing I said to him. Hossam looked relieved. As I left the hospital I heard him laughing. He had understood.

Hossam kept dreaming about both himself and the boy he had been. And I didn't smuggle in the Colt revolver for him. So he didn't use a revolver in the dream – he used a knife. A fellow patient had provided him with it. Hossam took the knife and slowly advanced towards Hossam the child, who was sitting in the dream director's chair, saying, 'I don't like this.' He was holding a bag of tangerines but he hadn't yet had a chance to taste one. Hossam came up to him, stuck his hand in the bag and took out a tangerine. With his other hand he planted the knife in the boy's neck. The boy shuddered like a hen that's had hot water poured on it, then fell off the chair, dead, without having a chance to wake up from the dream. Meanwhile everyone else in the dream took flight and they probably all woke up from their dreams at that moment. This is exactly what happened. Literally. I assure you. I know all the details: the lighting, how the child gasped for breath and gave up the ghost, even the colour of the knife handle. I know everything. Everything. Even the taste of the tangerines in the bag – I know it well. Because I was there.

Aquarium

WE CALLED HIM MUNIR, BUT HE WAS NO MORE than a lump of clotted blood in her womb. The doctor decided that it was a pregnancy. This was supported by the fact that my fiancée's stomach was swollen, she hadn't had her period, and she had pains in her ovaries. The swelling in her stomach wasn't really the result of a pregnancy, however. It was an inflammation caused by the interaction of several birth-control pills. Three times in succession, for example, she had taken 'morning after' pills, each of which cost thirty dollars.

We hadn't known each other long and we hadn't intended to have sex so soon. But sex saved our relationship. My fiancée insisted I show her my penis. She loved me very much but she was worried my penis might not be thick enough. She wasn't interested in the length, only in the girth. 'If it's thin, I won't be able to marry you,' she said. So my penis, and not my feelings, had the final say in our relationship. We were in the car and we stopped on the motorway. The street lamps were either burned out or turned off. In the car it wasn't possible to turn on the little ceiling light, and since my fiancée couldn't see my penis, she started groping it with her hand. Then she said, 'I think it's shaped like a kind of mushroom.' For a moment I didn't know whether this was a criticism of my penis, or praise. But she didn't give me a chance to ask. She pounced on it with her mouth, which took me by surprise and made me ejaculate. So we argued. My fiancée got out of the car, hailed a taxi and drove off. Then she sent me a text message saying, 'It's all over between us. Our relationship ended as quickly as you ejaculated.' I had to persuade her to try again. 'In bed things will be different,' I wrote to her, and so they were.

We had sex to save our emotional relationship. Daily for ten days. On each of the first three days my fiancée took a 'morning after' pill. Later she told me about a British lover of hers who had a very thin penis. 'It was as thin as a Bic biro,' she said. He used two of his fingers to supplement his penis. He wrapped them around his penis and put them in with it. My wife thought he had inserted a screw made of flesh and blood between her thighs. Every time he'd change the two fingers. He was well-practised at that. Sometimes he would cry. He'd stop having sex suddenly and go into a long monologue about how he wished he could have a thicker penis, so he wouldn't need to use his fingers. She told me he had volunteered to work with some humanitarian organization in Iraq and she no longer knew anything about him.

Munir wasn't a modern name. My fiancée and I knew that. We chose it initially as a joke, in the hope that the foetus was male. Then we believed it was male. The personality of the lump of gooey blood was male – that's what we decided. Then our relationship with him developed, so much so that sometimes I would wake up in the night to massage my fiancée's stomach with circular clockwise movements. Just to make sure that Munir was settled peacefully. But I wasn't aware I was doing this. In the morning, as soon as she woke up, my fiancée would hug me and say, 'Thank you, my dear.' And I would ask, 'For what?' 'For being such a good father,' she replied. Then I realized I had been sleepwalking. It didn't happen just the once – it recurred five or six times, until I started taking half a tablet of Lexotanil so that I didn't wake up during the night to touch Munir.

My fiancée concluded that I wouldn't be a good husband unless I sleepwalked. 'I wouldn't mind if you raised the children – all our children – when you're sleep-walking,' she joked. I didn't like the joke at the time. But now that some years have passed, I'd be more than willing to look after all our children while sleepwalking – I mean our children that have never come, and will never come.

Munir, that lump of clotted blood, wasn't destined to survive. We had to get him out of my fiancée's womb one day before the wedding. That was because his presence had caused her stomach to swell, which would have been seen as a scandal. But we hesitated. We argued often. The doctor herself wasn't sure whether the mysterious lump was a foetus or just clotted blood. My fiancée thought we had no right to remove a child from its place of residence. 'A child?' I said scornfully. 'At the moment it's no more important than the blood in a nosebleed or the blood that comes with piles.'

We sought the advice of a group of married friends, but none of them had experience of such a mystery in a womb. But the doctor settled the matter with a phone call, at eleven o'clock in the evening. 'I won't take responsibility,' she said angrily. 'If it sticks to the wall of the womb it might cause cancer.' Then she hung up.

That night I didn't take any Lexotanil, and indeed the next morning my fiancée told me, as we were getting dressed to go to the hospital, that I had got up during the night, sleepwalking of course, and had started massaging her stomach with circular movements. 'You even cried,' she added. I argued with her, saying, 'I'm going to ask you one question: do you enjoy having sex with me?' I interrupted her as she nodded her head: 'I enjoy it too – I love it. There'll definitely be another Munir, and we'll call him Munir, and I say that quite seriously.'

We kept Munir in a test tube. When I looked at him in the test tube the first time, I had a feeling he was exhausted. That was straight after the operation. During the operation the doctor couldn't contain her emotion when she scraped the clot of blood out of my fiancée's womb. She said a little 'yes' and her eyes filled with tears, confident that what lay on the scalpel in front of her was not a foetus. As she handed the test tube to us, she said, 'It's just a clot of blood. You can get rid of it however you see fit. Have a good look at it, just to be sure.' To be honest, I couldn't tell the difference. In the very earliest stages of its development you can tell a foetus from a blood clot only by feeling, and my feeling was that this solid clot of blood in the test tube was Munir. But I didn't say anything to my fiancée. I was bitterly disappointed. She, on the other hand, closed her eyes, fell asleep in the front seat of the car and didn't utter a word. I tucked the test tube into the glovebox where we keep CDs, turned the key in the ignition, and off we drove.

I don't remember being fascinated by a clot of blood before. Not before Munir. One rarely finds coagulated blood magical or enchanting. The globs of blood that we see on television have usually congealed under particularly wretched circumstances. If I were to be one hundred per cent objective, even Munir was ugly to look at. His structure was no different from that of any other blood clot taken from someone's leg or intestines or the phlegm in their throat. In the heaven where dried lumps of blood go, you'd find Munir wandering around aimlessly. There was nothing distinctive about him. If he held up a sign saying, 'I was extracted from a womb,' none of his fellow clots of blood would believe him. But what fascinated me about him was that he was pure. I don't know how to explain it.

Munir had panache. Charisma. Whenever I looked at him in the test tube, I'd find him cheerful. Like a small piece of liver, a fresh black piece, ready for grilling at a barbeque. He was dark red in colour and clear, as if he'd never been exposed to the air or to the bacteria in the womb.

Now he's lying low in formaldehyde. He spent some time in the small test tube in our sitting room. No one noticed that he was a clot of blood or that he was called Munir, unless we drew attention to it, because you don't find anyone displaying a lump of dry blood in his sitting room as if it were a brass or ceramic vase, or a bowl bought at a tourist shop. Some of our friends said they wished they could have kept something from their relatives who had died in explosions or traffic accidents or had disappeared in the war. A piece of flesh from their calf, perhaps, or a fingertip, or even a fingernail or an anklebone. In the living room we camouflaged Munir by surrounding his test tube with similar test tubes containing water and worthless pieces of blue, red and green plastic. Every week we changed the solution in Munir's test tube. It was a delicate and exhausting process, like changing his nappy or his clothes.

We later decided that the test tube no longer suited him, so we moved him to a larger container: an aquarium. It was a big aquarium, one designed to hold salmon. We set up the aquarium as the centrepiece in the living room instead of the forty-five-inch plasma television we had bought several years earlier, to watch football matches, and sometimes films, including porn. I have to say that the place did smell of formaldehyde, the solution preserving Munir, although we closed the aquarium tight. That meant that our friends and relatives rarely visited us. Sometimes we had to put masks on or leave the windows open, no matter whether it was sunny or rainy, or if there was shooting going on outside.

On 28 August Munir will be a year older, so we'll have a party. We've been doing this ever since Munir was eight, specifically since we found out that my wife's womb was irreparably damaged in the operation and will never be able to carry a foetus again.

Every year we invite children who share Munir's birthday to the party. We post this notice on the Internet: 'If you were born on 28 August, you are invited to celebrate your birthday at our house for free. Don't forget to invite your friends and relatives. The address is . . .' All the children we've invited gather at our house, together with their friends and relatives. We give them token presents, cut a cake for them and sing 'Happy Birthday to You'. All within sight of Munir, who's stuck to the glass at the front of the aquarium, as if watching sadly. Whenever one of the children asks us in disgust about this smudge on the glass – and we can't blame them for that, of course – we tell them the truth. We hear some of their relatives whispering things like, 'They must be mentally retarded. They're keeping a lump of blood in an aquarium.' But my wife and I have agreed that in reply we say, 'That's our son Munir. We invited you to our house because today is his birthday too.' Then we ask everyone to sing for Munir, as he sang for them from inside the aquarium. 'Happy birthday to you, happy birthday to you, happy birthday, dear Munir, happy birthday to you,' we sing along with the children, who are puzzled that there is a lump of blood in an aquarium meant for salmon.

This used to happen on 28 August every year, when the guests could still see Munir in the aquarium. But now they can't. That's because Munir ran into a problem.

He's no longer visible. At first we thought it was just a temporary indisposition. If Munir had been a fully grown child, we could definitely have found treatment for him. But because he was just a lump of dried blood, that was difficult. How can you save a lump of dried blood from shrinking? That's what happened. Munir started to shrink.

It began a few years ago. Every day he lost a bit of himself. A few cells. At first we didn't notice anything. But we were shocked when one of the children at the party said, 'Munir was bigger last year,' and showed us an old picture of Munir on his mobile phone.

Our boy went on like this until there wasn't a single blood cell left. My wife and I couldn't do anything. We called in doctors and experts to examine him. But they made it clear that they were helpless. Their answer was always the same: 'This isn't a child. This is a lump of clotted blood. Do you really want treatment for a lump of clotted blood?' So we gave in. All we could do was try psychiatry. We brought a famous psychiatrist to our house and explained the situation to him. 'Do you really think that psychiatry can treat a frustrated lump of clotted blood?' he said scornfully, looking at the aquarium in disgust. Then we decided to take Munir out into the wilderness, because we thought that in the aquarium Munir must have acquired animal characteristics.

My wife and I resigned from our jobs. We sold our little flat and the furniture, packed the pots and pans we needed into our car, plus some basic foodstuffs and tinned goods, and hired a pickup truck designed for carrying sheets of glass. The truck carried the aquarium with Munir, who was now invisible. When we arrived, we were exhausted. We put the aquarium in the open in the sunlight and lay down in front of it on a blanket that we spread on the grass.

The weather was beautiful and all we could hear around us were the soft sounds of that well-known conflict between the insects and the birds, to which no one pays any attention. But as we looked at the aquarium in the hope that Munir would start to take shape again, we dozed off. In my sleep I dreamed that wild animals arrived, surrounded the aquarium, and started to drink the formaldehyde in which Munir had spent the recent years of his life. I tried to fend them off by throwing unopened tins of food at them, while my wife started spraying them with water from the bottles we had brought with us. The strange thing was that my wife had the same dream. We discussed the colours and the details and even the sounds that the animals made and we found they were identical. There wasn't a single difference between the two dreams. 'It can't possibly be just a dream,' she said. 'It's a vision.' Shivers ran down our spines. We tried to pick up the aquarium and move it, but we couldn't. We couldn't budge it. How had the aquarium suddenly become so heavy? The only answer we could think of was that Munir didn't want to move out of the wilderness. That's what made us stay. For the rest of our lives all we have to look forward to is taking turns to guard the aquarium night and day and protect Munir. We no longer hope that he will grow to become a child one day, but just that he will go back to how we always knew him. We don't want more than that.

Portion of Jam

DAD COMES HOME HOLDING A LITTLE PLASTIC portion of jam like the ones they give the patients in the hospital where he works. He holds it up in the air and says, 'See the jam?'

'No,' I reply.

He puts his hand a little closer to the only lightbulb in the ceiling. 'And now?'

'No, I can't see anything,' I say.

'Maybe the lightbulb's too weak.'

'Maybe,' I say.

With a flourish that one has to admire, he makes the portion of jam roll down from between his fingers and settle in the palm of his hand. His closes his fist so that it looks like an envelope – an old trick he invented at nursing school. Now his hand is an envelope with the little portion of jam inside it. He presses the light switch with the edge of the envelope and the light goes out.

Then he presses the switch again and the light comes on.

Dad holds the jam up in the air again. 'Is this better?' he asks.

'No, I can't see any jam from where I am,' I say.

'Come a little closer. You're in the furthest possible spot in the room.'

He puts his hand closer to the light as if he's going to do another trick – making the portion of jam go right inside the lightbulb.

I am in fact a long way from Dad. I'm sitting on a chair next to the window. The chair is high and when I sit on it my feet don't touch the floor.

I get off the chair and move towards my father. 'Dad, can you put the jam inside the lightbulb?' I ask. 'If you put it inside the lightbulb, I could see it.'

He lifts his hand higher but before I reach him the power goes off. The darkness swallows Dad. It swallows his hand and the jam.

'See what happens when we put jam in the lightbulb?' he jokes. 'The packaging explodes, the jam burns and turns the whole room black.'

Transfixed, I say nothing.

Dad says nothing for a while either. Then he says, 'Go and flip the trip switch.'

'OK, I'll go and flip the trip switch,' I say, repeating his own words to reassure him.

I move forward with heavy steps, as if I have a tortoise clinging to each foot. I poke the darkness with my finger. It's like an animal that I'll tickle so that it shows me its stomach. I lift up one foot and bring the tortoise down on the animal's stomach. I lift up my other foot and bring down the other tortoise, and make my escape.

But then my finger hits Dad. He jumps and drops the portion of jam. 'Did you hear that? That's the sound of the jam!' he says excitedly, disguising his fear. But in fact I can't hear the sound of the jam, which rolls along the floor until it comes to a stop.

Dad doesn't move from where he is. He doesn't want to lose the jam, although our house is small – just one room plus a kitchen and a bathroom. But between our little room and the kitchen and the bathroom, there's another room, the biggest room in the house. Dad has rented that room to one of his relatives, who we found out was an arms dealer. Dad's relative brings home loads of weapons and ammunition. Sometimes he stands by the door of his room and, instead of saying 'good morning' to Dad, he says, 'What do you think of this piece? It's just a sample. It's a piece that's easy to use. It's from Romania. It has excellent sights. Why don't you borrow it for a day or two? Don't you have any disputes with anyone?' Dad has never owned a gun, and the only dispute he has is with this relative of his, who has stopped paying the rent. But Dad doesn't dare ask him for it. Dad thinks that the relative should not only pay him rent but also take out a mortgage.

In his other hand, the hand that wasn't holding up the portion of jam, Dad's holding a bag. A bag with lots of tissues inside. His passport too. And a party official's card. Dad sees the card as a weapon, his only weapon. Sometimes he leaves the card on a stool near the door so that his relative can see it clearly.

'When you've flipped the trip switch, come back through this door,' Dad whispers. He puts his hand into the bag and picks out the card. He does a turn of about 270 degrees towards the door of his relative's room, from where one can hear the sound of weapons being loaded and unloaded. Dad doesn't trust his relative. 'Do you think he's inside?' he asks me.

The jam has come to rest at the relative's door.

'Maybe,' I say, though the words hardly make it out of my throat. I conclude that I'm also frightened.

Dad and I both know that the relative is in his room. Dad could have turned ninety degrees instead of 270 degrees. It occurs to me that he wanted to come with me to flip the trip switch, but then he remembered the jam.

The fuse box is in the kitchen, so in order to reach it I have to leave our room through a side door – a door that leads to the corridor on the ground floor where we live, and from that corridor I have to come into the house through the front door, where you find the kitchen and the bathroom. 'Shut the door quietly and don't be long,' Dad says.

There are rats in the building, and they like to sneak into houses in the dark. I open the door a fraction and sidle out, kicking the air at ground level to frighten off the rats if there are any there. I shut the door quietly, as Dad requested, so as not to annoy the relative, though we don't know if he's alone in his room or has someone with him.

I feel my way along the wall of the corridor and come to the front door of our house. I take out the key that I always keep in my pocket. I open the door and sidle into the house, aiming several swift kicks at the air near the floor, but behind me this time. I approach the fuse box, touch the switch and push it down, but the power from the generator doesn't come back on. Now I'm in the kitchen, while Dad remains immobile in our room. Between him and me lies the relative's room, which Dad and I are banned from entering, and the relative can come into the kitchen directly through a door from his room.

I can't speak to Dad from here because I'd have to raise my voice and that might upset our relative, who might be doing business with one of his clients. So I can either go back to our room and wait with Dad for the power from the generator to come back on, or I can stay in the kitchen, switching back and forth between the mains and the generator, or I can go and pay the bill for the generator, because the owner of the generator might have cut us off for not paying it. Of course it's not a good time to pay the bill because it's II o'clock in the evening. I can't see Dad from where I am in the kitchen and he can't see me either. After I don't know how many minutes, the relative comes out of his room, with a gun in his hand, because he feels hot. That's what he does when he feels hot – he picks up his gun and comes out. He's about to say angrily, 'This piece is smuggled, smuggled from Israel,' but he treads on the jam. The portion of jam splits open and splatters his foot with sticky apricot jam, so he opens fire.

My father no longer goes to the hospital to work, because you don't find nurses in wheelchairs working in hospitals. But he's made a deal with a colleague, who brings him little portions of jam twice a week. He can't stand up, and he can't even push his wheelchair with his hands. But he looks up towards the lightbulb whenever he sees me coming into the room. I'm no longer a child, though. Inside the lightbulb I find a portion of jam. 'How did you do that?' I ask him. But Dad doesn't answer because, just as he can't walk or move his hands, he can't speak either. He smiles. I try to reach the jam but I realize it's impossible, because the lightbulb's too high and the only person in the house who can bring it down is our relative, with a bullet from his revolver.

Curtain

OUR BED IS NEAR THE BALCONY DOOR, AND THE balcony door has a curtain. My wife likes to leave the door open and pull the curtain closed when we have sex. Our flat is on the seventh floor and it can be windy up here. The wind comes in through the window and goes out through the door. It moves the curtain a little. Our neighbour, an elderly dwarf, watches us from the building opposite and shouts, 'There's someone fucking on the seventh floor.' All the people come out of their flats and stand on their balconies. Our neighbour says it in a loud voice but in a solemn tone, as if he's in a literary salon. He doesn't even look in our direction when he announces his discovery.

Nothing stops me when I'm fucking. I can't. If I stopped, it would put me in a bad mood for the rest of the day. It would also have a negative effect on my wife, who's so sensitive she says she wants a divorce whenever I say anything that offends her. So what I do is I ask her to hold the curtain and pull it down when we're having sex. That way we make sure the wind won't lift the curtain up. But when my wife reaches orgasm, she clenches her thighs and her fists as tight as she can, and her body becomes twice as heavy. On one occasion she pulled the curtain down when she reached orgasm and it came off the rail. This was seen by the old dwarf, who apparently has nothing to do all day but spy on us. He shouted out, 'The woman's having an orgasm!' and people flocked to their balconies like maniacs and started looking in our direction and making comments. Some of them even said, 'Wow! What a stud!' One of them clapped and another one whistled.

I suggested to my wife that we simply keep the balcony door closed but she refused. She has a good reason. 'When it gets hot, my husband, you can't keep going for long, can you?' she said. This is true. And there's no electricity in the neighbourhood most of the time, so there's no solution other than to change the curtain or change the neighbours.

I've thought about threatening the dwarf, or getting revenge on him. He's ruined the moments that are dearest to my heart, the moments when I am having sex with my wife. Anyway, we decided to change the curtain for a thicker one. At the same time I made up my mind to visit the dwarf and speak to him calmly about the problem.

The man has never married. That may be why he's so interested in other people's business. He doesn't have a job either. At the end of every month he receives some money from one of his brothers in the United States. His brothers have suggested that he move there, but he refuses. He says he really loves this city, and since he discovered that the young couple who recently moved into the area have sex two or sometimes three times a day, he never leaves the balcony. He carries a walking stick and the doctor has advised him to walk. You can see him walking up and down the balcony instead of going downstairs to walk along the seafront, because he doesn't want to miss a single moment of the sex show, which is much more important as far as he's concerned. But the balcony is small and he misjudged the distance, walking much further than he would have walked on the seafront. After two weeks, his legs felt tired, very tired. They did an operation on him but it didn't work and now he can't walk without the aid of a Zimmer frame. He no longer carries a stick and he's slower.

Two or three weeks ago a fire broke out in the big house where he lives alone and it destroyed all his furniture and possessions. The little man only just managed to escape. But he did survive and he thanked the Lord.

Then he sent a message to his brothers, who quickly sent him some money. Since the fire, he hasn't appeared on the balcony and I heard that he was accusing me of laying a curse on him, saying that the whole fire was to take revenge on him for spying on us and trying to cause scandals for me and my wife.

In fact I was worried about him, and so was my wife. When we had sex, we would pull the thick curtain open a little (the wind could no longer move it), to see whether the dwarf was on the balcony or not. Maybe we had grown accustomed to his voice, or his voice had become a catalyst for sex between us. But we started talking about the dwarf when we were in bed, instead of cuddling and playing around. We started asking each other what might have happened to him, and after a while we were no longer able to have sex.

My wife insisted we go and visit him, so we went and knocked on the door of his house. He was surprised to see us and asked us in. The walls of the house still showed signs of the fire. He offered us some fruit juice and started apologizing and crying. 'Forgive me. See what God has done to me,' he said. We told him we weren't angry with him. But he wasn't convinced until, when we were leaving the house, I whispered in his ear, 'Do you want me to show you proof that we aren't angry with you?' His eyes lit up and he nodded, saying,

'As you wish, but it's your own responsibility. I'm not responsible.'

I smiled.

The next day we waited till he came out on the balcony and then we started to have sex. We had put back the old curtain, the thin one, and sure enough, as soon as the first breeze blew, we heard the dwarf shouting, 'There's someone fucking on the seventh floor. They're fucking just for me. Don't go out on your balconies, you sons of bitches.'

Juan and Ausa

IF I HADN'T MET JUAN I WOULD HAVE MISSED THE most pleasant experiences I've ever had. He is married to Ausa and this is how they met:

Ausa was living at the time in a town in Spain, in a small ground-floor flat on a narrow street called Pablo Gargallo. Its only window looked directly onto the street. Ausa didn't know that they held a bull run in the street once a year – you know, one of those fiestas where they goad a bull and it charges at everyone it sees in front of it. Juan was a young man who was eager to take part in the fiesta. You don't have to pay to run with the bull. All you have to do is challenge the bull and then try your hardest to get out of the way when it tries to dig its horns into your chest.

Juan was no expert, as he had never taken part in such an event before. That morning Juan had had sex with his neighbours' daughter. He hadn't washed his hands so the smell of her vagina clung to his fingers. Juan spent the morning walking through the crowded streets, putting his hands to his face and smelling his fingers. It was the first time he had had sex. 'That day I achieved three objectives all at once,' he told me. It was the first time he had had sex, it was the first time he had run with a bull in Pablo Gargallo Street, and he was about to meet Ausa. What happened was that the bull singled him out from all the others, not because of his virility but because of the smell that lingered under his fingernails. Juan turned his back on the bull and started to run, as he was meant to. He was enthusiastic, but also frightened. This competition wasn't like previous competitions: the person the bull was chasing had to wrap some sticky tape around the bull's horns. If he failed, he lost and his reputation as a real man would be damaged.

The organizers had given out rolls of sticky tape to the public and asked them to throw the rolls to the person that the bull chose to chase. The man (in this case Juan) was meant to catch one of these rolls, undo the tape and wrap it around the bull's horns, which meant he had to stop running every now and then and turn around to see the bull.

What happened was that the smell of sex made the bull angry and it didn't give Juan a chance to catch his breath. Juan started running as fast as he could, clutching the sticky tape nervously in his hand. Even the people felt sorry for him because the enraged animal, which weighed about eight hundred kilos, pursued him relentlessly. He jumped off a little ledge, climbed on top of a pile of rubbish and ran along a wall, but the bull wouldn't leave him alone. All Juan could do was throw himself through Ausa's open window, from where she was watching the fiesta. It's a good omen, of course, to have a handsome man jump through your window, but you may well panic when you see a bull coming in behind him. Ausa told me that she hid in the small cupboard under the sink, leaving Juan and the bull to fight it out in the flat. The cupboard was smashed, the bed was broken and when the bull snagged the chandelier with its horns it fell to the floor and shattered, along with a valuable collection of ceramics that Ausa had put together from various places in Spain. Incandescent with rage, she came out of her hiding place in the kitchen and grabbed a large knife. She made straight for the bull, head to head, and sank the knife into its shoulder with a sideways thrust. The animal fell to the floor. Seizing his opportunity, Juan pounced on the wounded bull and wrapped the sticky tape around its horns.

People had now gathered at the window, but none of them saw what happened, because everything that Ausa and Juan did to the bull took place in the corridor.

It took thirteen men to remove the bull from the flat. Its horns were covered in sticky tape and blood was running down its neck and head. People thought Juan was a hero.

Juan promised Ausa he would repair all the damage the bull had done and he did indeed spend more than two weeks fixing the cupboard and the window frame that the bull's hooves had ruined. The work on the flat should have taken less than two weeks, but Juan worked slowly and spoke a lot. He told Ausa everything about his life, except about the girl he had had sex with on the morning of the day he jumped through Ausa's window. Juan was thirty and Ausa was twenty-seven.

The people in Pablo Gargallo Street thought the bull must have been the brother of the girl Juan had slept with. In that town people believe that bulls and people can be brothers and sisters. If it hadn't been related, it wouldn't have been so angry. Now they had to find out the identity of the girl who was the bull's sister. The men threatened to hold Juan to account, so they brought all the girls out of their houses and told them to walk past the bull, which was standing in its pen covered in a large piece of cloth. The bull was supposed to identify the girl that Juan had had sex with. In fact, as soon as the girl walked towards the animal, it went up to her and lowed in her face. Her father promised to hang Juan within sight of the bull in the pen. Juan had to find a solution.

He denied the whole story to Ausa, cried and asked her to help. They spent a night thinking of a solution. Then at last they found it: Juan would marry the young girl and Ausa would marry the bull. Nominally, of course, because that was the best solution, because the people who lived in Pablo Gargallo Street asked the girl not to abandon her brother the bull and to look after it, to make up for the shame she had caused it. And so it was. A short time later, Juan, Ausa, the girl and the bull all boarded a small truck and left the neighbourhood.

On the way the bull started lowing and roaring because the swaying of the truck made its shoulder hurt. The wound hadn't completely healed yet. This upset the driver, who told them all to get out. After waiting some time on the motorway, Juan managed to hitch a ride with a driver. Ausa and Juan got into the car and asked the girl to wait with her brother the bull until Juan came back with a small truck. But Juan and Ausa left the girl and the bull and ran off. Since then they haven't heard anything about them. They got married and moved to live and work near me, as political activists.

My friendship with Juan only began when he saw me butting an old school blackboard with my horns. I was by myself and bored. My only aim was to have fun and show off my strength to some cats and some unemployed farm workers. That was shortly after the last war.

I had stopped going to the field because the farmer who was my master had died when a large piece of shrapnel from a shell had destroyed his liver.

Anyway, I never went back to turning the water-wheel. That was because Juan bought me from the farmer's children and moved me into the garden of his big house. Unlike other bulls, I don't have a rope around my neck. I'm always in the garden and all I do is listen to Juan's and Ausa's stories and put up with being pestered by the children – Ausa tells them to feed me guavas from behind the fence while she grooms me with soap and water. My view is that Juan and Ausa are idiots. Whenever Juan sees me lying down, he comes up and whispers, 'How's your sister?' I nod my head a few times, which he interprets to mean 'She's OK. She's on her way here with her father.' Ausa, on the other hand, is terrified at the prospect of the girl's father arriving, so they argue, and as usual I hear them discussing the question of executing me soon, but they daren't do that, of course, since I'm a bull. As for me, since I can't take part in the conversation, I get fed up. I chew some of the fruit that's been put beside me and go to sleep.

Anyway, I never went back to turning the water wheel. That was because Jatti bought me from the farmer's children and moved me into the garden of